Wild Chicory

Wild Chicory

KIM KELLY

First published in 2015 by Pan Macmillan
Republished in 2016 by The Author People

Cover image of girl by Douglas Frost, and image of chicory by Kim Kelly.

ISBN 9781922598141 (print)
ISBN 9781922598325 (ebook)

Published in Australia and New Zealand by:

Brio Books, an imprint of Booktopia Group Ltd
Unit E1, 3-29 Birnie Avenue
Lidcombe, NSW 2141, Australia

Printed and bound in Australia by SOS Print + Media Group

The paper in this book is FSC® certified. FSC® promotes environmentally responsible, socially beneficial and economically viable management of the world's forests.

MIX
Paper from responsible sources
FSC® C011217

Proudly Printed
In Australia

booktopia.com.au

For Geraldine,
daughter of Lillian,
mother of me

We must remain as close to the flowers, the grass, and the butterflies as the child is who is not yet so much taller than they are. . . Whoever would partake of all good things must understand how to be small at times.

Friedrich Nietzsche,
'The Wanderer and his Shadow'
Human, All Too Human: A book for free spirits, 1880

Had I the heavens' embroidered cloths,
Enwrought with golden and silver light,
The blue and the dim and the dark cloths
Of night and light and the half-light,
I would spread the cloths under your feet:
But I, being poor, have only my dreams;
I have spread my dreams under your feet;
Tread softly because you tread on my dreams.

W.B. Yeats,
'Aedh Wishes for the Cloths of Heaven'
The Wind Among the Reeds, 1899

GOOD WHITE BREAD

The good white bread comes in tubes, from town. Pipe loaves, they're called. My grandmother carefully slices down the faint pipe lines in the circle crust with her feather knife. The handle of the knife is the colour of a dog bone, and the feathers are steel teeth – they will shred your fingers, if you're not careful. The house is quiet downstairs; it's just me and Grandma here, up in her flat, in her kitchen.

'How do they get the bread out of the pipe?' I ask her. I'm wondering at the lines in the crust: they bump along the loaf like the pipe might be made out of corrugated iron – tiny corrugated iron, though. I can't work it out. 'Wouldn't it get stuck?'

'Don't addle me,' she says, slicing, slicing. Her hips sway at the kitchen bench, her elbow sawing, sawing. Every slice is exactly the same size; I can't imagine ever being able to do that.

She's making toast, for lunch. She always has two slices, which she butters and then squishes a whole banana between with the back of a fork, but she doesn't usually have the pipe loaf bread, the good white bread, just for this sort of everyday lunch if it's just us, and she's up to slice number eight now. I don't think we're expecting anyone to come round today. Maybe she's hungry. But I can't imagine that, either: she never eats more than what she calls an 'elegant sufficiency'. Mum says that just means she doesn't want to get fat. Mum always teases Grandma for being so vain, for being so slim and dyeing her hair. 'There's nothing wrong with taking care of your appearance,' Grandma would always laugh back. She is beautiful, my grandmother: she piles up her red curls so that squiggly tendrils frame her face and make her eyes bluer than blue, and she makes all her own clothes – she makes all of mine, too. She's always the most fashionable lady at mass. Today, she's wearing her lolly-pink skirt with the white stitching, and her pink-and-white-striped blouse. Normally, she giggles a lot, even at mass. It's the only time you can really see her wrinkles, when she giggles at something silly – especially when it's at something Father Jovanovic has said, but Mum says that's just because he's too handsome. Grandma's not even smiling now, though. She's very sad at the moment, so I'm not going to addle her. I'm trying to be quiet.

Granddad's never coming home again, that's why she's so sad. He had a stroke three Tuesdays ago, on his way home from work. He didn't have to go to work – he's retired. He only goes in to help the new man make sense of all the orders when it's busy. They work in a huge refrigerator, making sure that all the thousands of bottles of flavoured milk and cartons of yoghurt get on the trucks and into the shops and all get paid for. Well, Granddad used to, anyway. He used to bring home strawberry milk and apricot yoghurt – my favourites. That's not going to happen anymore.

I sleep in the big bed with Grandma now to keep Granddad's side from getting cold. No-one asked me to; I just do. I don't want her to read in bed alone. She reads doctor-and-nurse romance novels from the library, 'to give her brain a rest,' she says; and I read *Nancy Drew* detective mysteries – I'm collecting them. I love the name Nancy, it's so pretty. My name is Brigid, and I don't always like it. Bridge. Bridgey. Brigid. It's an old-fashioned name. 'A big name for a little girl,' Mum always says. It's a name I have to live up to. It's my grandmother's confirmation name, and my great-grandmother's Christian name, apart from being Saint Brigid's name in the first place. Brigid stands for being kind to the poor, healing sores, and, most importantly, being good at making cakes. I'm much more expert at licking the bowl clean – that's the fault of my middle name, Danielle, Grandma says.

I wish I could make her laugh right now.

I can't imagine how much she is missing Granddad. I miss him. I miss the rough way he rubbed my hair with the towel after Grandma washed it on Saturday afternoons. 'You'll rub her scalp off her head one day,' she would tell him from the kitchen. I would say, 'Ouch!' But I didn't mean it. I loved the way my head would bobble about in his big, rough hands, cigarette in the corner of his mouth, ash falling off the end and onto the carpet. Grandma says it's good for keeping the moths away – cigarette ash on the carpet. Mum says cigarettes killed Granddad. I heard her whispering it to Dad in the bathroom downstairs, when she went in there to have a cry.

I look down at the carpet now, into the orange-and-brown swirls under the chair I'm sitting on. It's Granddad's usual chair. He would sit here, on this side of the kitchen table, where there's lounge-room carpet on the floor, reading the newspaper, smoking his cigarette. I wonder how much cigarette ash is in there, in this bit of carpet. I look right under the table: there's not a speck of dust in the tiny lines that go along the strip of golden metal that divides off the lounge-room-carpet side from the kitchen-vinyl-tiles side. It's one long room up here in Grandma's flat, a lounge room with a kitchen at one end, where the stove and the sink and the cupboards are – she designed it all this way herself. When I sit up straight in the chair again, a line of sunlight is going across my knees, coming through the open slits in the blinds behind me. I swing my legs out from under the chair. My legs are skinny and brown; bruised and spotted with mosquito bites.

It's hot. I should go and play outside in the shade of the house, maybe see who's home over the road, see if Sharon is back from the shops yet, but I don't want to leave Grandma alone, not now while she's being so strange about the toast. It's school holidays, luckily, so I can be here at home with her. I don't normally like school holidays that much. It's so boring, especially the long summer holidays. It's too hot to think properly. But I'm glad it's holidays this time. Shane and Tim, my brothers, are at Aunty Jeannie and Uncle Vic's in Campbelltown, on the farm, probably playing cricket with our cousins there, Matt and Jason. I'm glad they're not here – they're too loud, always smashing around inside or outside. The yard is too small to get away from them, and they just get bigger and teenage-stinkier every day. Anyone would think there were ten of them, not two. I never want to go to high school, where there would be more than a hundred of them.

Over my shoulder, through the blinds, I look out past the back fence and across the iron rooftops all the way to town. We live up on the hill, in Marrickville, so we can see right into Sydney. Australia Square is round, a pipe loaf standing up out of the ground, with its corrugated bumps gone all wobbly in the heat – the whole city looks like it's melting. It's 1976, January something. Wednesday. Mr Whitlam made a sticky mess of things before Christmas and he's not Prime Minister anymore – he got the sack. Dad told Mum maybe that's what made Granddad have such a bad stroke.

'Oh you stupid—' Grandma's suddenly rousing at the sink. I turn back around and see the smoke curling up from the toaster. She's burnt the first lot of toast, and now she's grabbing it out to scrape off the charcoal into the sink with the flat back of the feather knife. She's angry as she does it: scraping, scraping. Scraping off the black.

'No, I am not wearing black,' is what she said on the morning of Granddad's funeral. She was angry then, much more angry. She said to the crucifix on the wall above the bed: 'Steven would never approve of my wearing black in any circumstance – we go our own way, always have, always will.' She didn't know I was watching as she prayed there on her knees at the end of the bed that morning; she was having an argument with God, it sounded like. I don't think she saw me at all for a couple of days. She probably didn't look at God, either. I wasn't allowed to go with her to the funeral, but I wish I could have. We always sit together at mass.

I wish I could make her happy again. Happy in her eyes, like the way she used to look at Granddad. We were all so happy at Christmas, just when the holidays started – Grandma bought Granddad some smart new handkerchiefs, and he really loved them even though they're only handkerchiefs. That was only five days before – it just doesn't seem fair.

'I don't mind the burnt ones,' I tell her now in a rush, and it's true, I like the burnt ones best – I like them with vegemite and no butter, so that Mum says I'm too fussy and Grandma says it's not being too fussy to know what you want. 'Save them for me. Please.'

I don't know if she heard me, though. She just stands there at the sink, staring at the wall, like she's looking for something in the daisy tiles there. She's looking for Granddad – I might be only nine years old, but I know that. I'm looking for him, too.

I'm looking for something to make Grandma turn around to see me. Something not silly. Something to take us away, somewhere else, far away. I know . . .

'Tell me the story about the little boy and the fire,' I ask her, and if she tells me to be quiet it doesn't matter. 'Tell me about little Pete, tell me the fire tale,' I ask her again, and I do want to hear the story. I've heard it ten times, probably, the fire tale. Fire tail: it makes me think of a dragon's tail right now, swirling orange and brown through the air, over the rooftops, swirling us backwards in time, to the days when she was a girl. A little girl called Nell. 'Tell me about when you were small. Please, Grandma?'

But still she doesn't say anything. She puts the kettle on, and then she lights her cigarette. I think maybe I should make lunch for Grandma, rather than the other way round, but before I go to get up off the chair to do that, she turns to me, and she smiles. It's sad, but it's a smile, and I smile back at her.

THE FIRE TAIL

Peter Daniel Kennedy was the last of fourteen children and the thirteenth boy. Lucky Pete, they all called him, because they all loved him and, because of that, he was spoiled. He was the plumpest little boy that ever was, and the first of the Kennedys to be born in sunny Sydney. His face was the sun, ringed with strawberry curls.

His oldest brother, Dan, was twenty-two years his elder, and he would toss little Pete up in the air as soon as looking at him, toss him round the kitchen table and up the hall to all his brothers: Mick, Pat, Frankie, Chris, Ben, Dom, Sean, Martin, Eddie, Tom and Jack. In among all the boots and knees and elbows squashed into their little house in Surry Hills, was Nell – the real thirteenth and the only girl – but she was a whole other story in herself, and one for another time.

It was the happiest home anyone could ever hope to have, but no easy life for any in it, for Pete's family, the Kennedys, were very poor – when it came to money, if not love and laughter, that is. His parents – being his mother, Brigid, and his father, who was also called Dan – had spent every penny they owned bringing all their children all the way from Ireland on the long journey across the sea to Australia. All except lucky little Pete, of course – he was born the year they arrived, on the seventeenth of September 1912. It's true that his mother cried for the first three days after his birth, wondering how on earth she was going to keep her fourteenth and very much unexpected miracle when she could barely keep the other thirteen, but on that third day, a different kind of miracle was brought to her and her family: her husband, Dan – Mr Kennedy – finally got a good job.

Up until then, Dan the father and Dan the son, as well as the elder brothers Mick and Pat, and occasionally the first lot of twins Frankie and Chris, had had only piecemeal work labouring here and there, at this odd job and that, sweeping floors or lumping sacks. Sometimes they trapped rats for the Board of Public Health, getting a farthing a tail. They'd go rabbit hunting, too, out past the city, and at least what they didn't sell they could bring home to Mother. So this good new job of Dan the father's was a precious thing for the Kennedys. He was working now for the Eveleigh railway yards, over the tracks in Redfern, six days a week and regular hours, with money enough to pay the rent and most of the grocery bill – he even had to join the union, and pay them, too. It wasn't the best job – he was only coaling and stoking the furnaces in the locomotive workshop as assistant to the blacksmiths there – but it was a start. It was the answer to their prayers. It's true that he coveted a place in the workshop as a blacksmith, for that had been his trade back in Ireland, where he'd even had his own forge, but he'd never got his ticket to say that's what he was for he'd never before had to leave his village to get one. He didn't mind too much, though; he was a patient man – he had to be with all those children. And he believed if he worked hard enough, and prayed hard enough, he soon would be a blacksmith again.

Only it wasn't to be. On the nineteenth of September, 1913, just one year and two days after little Pete was born, Dan the father was crossing the road at Regent Street, on his way home from work at Redfern to Surry Hills, just thinking of his dinner, just thinking of the way all his babies and boys would jostle and jabber around the table, all happy with good food in their bellies, when a runaway team of horses dragging a cart piled high with sacks of chicory root put an end to all his hopes and dreams. There was bedlam in the street when it happened, screaming and shouting, and the carter was going mad that his load had tipped over, shaking his fists in the air and crying that his chicory was all smashed and worthless now. No-one in the street was paying any attention to the carter, though. They were all screaming and shouting for Dan Kennedy, for he was killed, his poor head broken under that wild stamping of hooves. He was forty-four years old.

Dan the son stepped up and took on the role of head of the household as best he could, continuing to labour at this job and that, mostly lumping sacks of wheat off the Pyrmont wharves across town, but it was never enough to feed such a family of fifteen mouths altogether. Young Dan could do no better, though: he had no ticket for a trade himself, either, and no good education to speak of, beyond the very basics of reading and writing and arithmetic. Before they'd left Ireland, he'd walk seven miles into Tralee to lump cargo for the ships in the canal there, but when the docks at Fenit Harbour opened with the railways, he wasn't needed so much anymore. He'd walk into Tralee, just as he'd walk into Pyrmont now, hoping, praying, for a day's work. If it weren't for the sunshine of Sydney, and Lucky Pete's sunny little face to come home to, some days Dan felt he might as well chuck himself into the sea. Not that he would ever truly do a thing like that – no, he would never do a sinful thing like that to his mother.

Brigid Kennedy worked hard herself, at keeping the home run smartly, and doing her own best to bring in what pennies she could. It was the only thing she could do against all her grief. She took in sewing and mending for the neighbours, and minding babies in the front room of their too-little house on Great Buckingham Street, but that didn't add much to their income, either – it would barely pay for a basket of old bread, especially as Brigid Kennedy's heart was too often too big and too fond of babies to charge the poor mothers needing baby-minding anything at all. At the heart of her heart, though, she knew she had too many fine sons to worry all that much. Their fortunes would surely change.

And so they did. Dan, Mick and Pat – the eldest three together – soon came up with an idea. What they lacked in education they made up for in plain old-fashioned brains. They were smart lads, shrewd and charming all, tall and handsome, too, with great big blue eyes, every single one – although none would marry before they saw their mother's life made easier. It came to their attention that one of the old houses in nearby Elizabeth Lane had been condemned by Public Health – a rickety wreck of a thing with 'DO NOT ENTER' painted across its boarded up windows – and, as poverty is the true mother of invention, so they decided it would be the ideal place to set up a betting shop. This shop was the kind where men from the neighbourhood could come to have a little gamble on the horse races, or a quiet game of swy – which was a coin-tossing game – but since this was all quite against the law of the day, they needed a place such as the little tumble-down house on Elizabeth Lane to conduct their business. It was so perfect, this little house, the wooden floor was so rotten out the back they didn't even have to bother putting a trapdoor in – if the police ever came, they could all just jump down through the holes in the boards to get away.

The betting shop was an instant success, and men would come from a mile all around and at all hours, to play their games. Sometimes the Kennedy boys made so much money they had to hide it from their mother so she wouldn't worry how they might have got it. As it was, Brigid did worry a little; she had her suspicions, not least by the whispers of gossip that swept from privy to privy along the back lane, but she knew better than to ask her sons about it in this instance. Whatever they were doing when they left her care, their endeavours had meant they could all move to a bigger house, up on Crown Street. It meant never more than three to a bed now. It meant they could all stay together for as long as they could imagine. It meant Dom could take a boilermaker's apprenticeship going at the gasworks; then Frankie and Chris got work at the post office running telegrams; then Ben got accepted into the technical college to learn to be a draughtsman. It meant a little bit of respectability, too, for even though the new house was still in Surry Hills, it was in a better part of that suburb.

With that little bit of respectability, though, came a higher price in bigotry and the strife such thinking brings. It's strange how that happens, isn't it? With a little bit of ease in one thing comes a little bit more difficulty in another. At least that's the way it usually is for the poor. Brigid Kennedy, in leaving a neighbourhood where everyone fairly much sat at the bottom of the barrel, suddenly found herself in a place where the snipes and nasty whispers down the back lane moved up to the front fences of the street and could do real and terrible harm. Most of their neighbours now, in the bigger terraces of Crown Street near where it crossed Cleveland, were Protestants, while the Kennedys, of course, remained as Roman Catholic as they ever were. As Brigid was quite bigoted herself, she didn't mind all that much on her own account whatever they might have said as she passed by on her way to the grocer or to the butcher. Any person of intelligence must respect an adversary to pay their judgement any heed, mustn't they? What she did mind was her children being subject to any prejudice, especially from those she considered to be godless heathens, and whenever it occurred, as it did now with some regularity, it would send her into a fury.

All of the little ones still at school – that was the second twins, Sean and Martin, then Eddie, Tom, Jack and little Nell – had to run the gauntlet home through enemy territory every afternoon from the corner of Devonshire Street, where their school sat. The first block along Crown Street was all right, but the second, after Lansdowne Street, was where the trouble began. The Upton children at number 636, and the Boyles at 640, would lie in wait for the Kennedys, pelting rocks at them as they passed on their way to number 654. Inevitably, one little Kennedy would bound in the door bawling and Brigid would bound out, banging on one of those neighbours' doors: 'I know you're in there Johnny Upton – you come out now and try throwing your rocks at me!' She'd only get one of their mothers opening the door to say: 'My little Johnny has been indoors practising the piano all afternoon.'

Brigid Kennedy would want to throw a piano at that other mother, and if she'd have had one handy, she might have.

The only one who never came home bawling was little Nell. She might have been younger and smaller than all her brothers except for the baby, Lucky Pete, she might have been only seven then, but she gave as good as she got. She would get mad as her mad red hair and yell back at the Uptons or the Boyles, or the whole lot of them: 'Catholics, Catholics ring the bell, Protestants, Protestants go to hell!' If they made fun of the farm-girl County Kerry way she spoke, she would make fun of the way they did, too: 'Go back to Belfast – you mouldy orange heads,' or to the Boyles in particular: 'Go and burst yourselves.' She would pull faces and stick her tongue out and tell them the Devil would take their brains out through their noses in the night with a long needle – and it would be easy work as their brains were so tiny and slippery. She would light up one of her older brothers' cigarettes and blow smoke in their faces right through their front gate. But there was one thing Nell Kennedy would never do: she would never, ever throw a rock, or a stick, or a stone at anyone. You might take their eye out, mightn't you, and she didn't want anything like that on her conscience.

A couple of years rolled on, and the rocks thrown by the Protestants only got worse: rocks coming right through Catholics' windows now with a Great War in Europe begun between Britain and France on one side, and Germany and who knew who else on the other, all a world away. Sinn Feiners – republican traitors – that's what they called every Irish Catholic now in Surry Hills, and if they could have invented a law to lock them all up in Darlinghurst Gaol just for being themselves, they would have. As it was, they sent the Child Welfare people to Brigid Kennedy's door on a bogus charge of head lice – bogus because no lice would be brave enough or foolish enough to resist her fine-tooth comb. But of greater and more serious importance, they finally got the police to close down the elder Kennedys' betting shop in Elizabeth Lane. The lads put their hands up immediately on this one, though. They'd had a good run of it; they'd had remarkably good relations with the police up until this time as well, but that's another story, too.

Dan, Mick and Pat were given a quiet choice by the authorities: Darlinghurst Gaol or the army – the Australian Imperial Forces. Either way, their mother was in a fury of all furies. She had worn only black since her husband had died, and black she would only ever wear: how dare her boys tempt further mourning: if she lost one of her children now, she would have to paint her soul black. For the time being, she threw her rolling pin at Mick and got him right in the middle of his forehead. But, as always, violence makes no difference to anything other than to make a bad situation worse. Brigid felt just dreadful for braining Mick, while Lucky Pete, who was now not yet four, cried and carried on for seeing it too, and her three eldest boys were set to leave her regardless. In the end the lads decided, for various practical reasons, that the army was the only sensible course. They thought that the food and the six shillings a day offered at Victoria Barracks in Paddington would be the better offer than nothing but cold porridge at Darlinghurst Gaol. And it was: they couldn't believe how well they'd landed when they got their soldiering kits: three caps, two pairs of boots, three pairs of socks, three pairs of breeches, two flannel shirts, two warm jackets and a great coat – each! As well as a toothbrush. Most of all, though, they thought they might bring some peace to the neighbourhood by going to war for England, too, to prove that not all poor and Irish Catholic boys were nought but Fenian thugs.

Off they marched to Circular Quay, so tall and handsome in their uniforms, with a brass band playing over a thousand mothers' tears and streamers streaming from the ship as it steamed away. Then afterwards, back at Crown Street, Frankie and Chris were soon moaning that they wanted to go, too, and their mother looked over at her rolling pin but, thinking the better of it, she told those younger boys outright that she would take her own life, commit the sin of all sins, if they ever did any such thing.

Despite all this, despite three sons off fighting a battle that wasn't theirs to fight, despite this noble sacrifice, peace did not come to Surry Hills, nor for the Kennedys.

One afternoon, not a fortnight since Dan and Mick and Pat had left, Nell came yelling up the hall from the front door: 'Mum! Mum! Mum!' She was holding her hand to the side of her head and blood was streaming from a wound.

'My girl! What have you done!' was Brigid's first response, for Nell being Nell, and ever more recklessly ten years old now, her mother has assumed she'd hit her head on the step while doing a cartwheel or something silly like that.

'Johnny Upton!' Nell shouted the house down as she ran into her mother's arms: 'That Johnny Upton! He got me with the biggest rock! I'll kill him one day!'

Brigid Kennedy stood there for a moment in shock: both that Johnny Upton had been so wicked as to injure another child in this way, and that her own daughter had expressed such a murderous desire for revenge. But then, with Nell's blood flowing all down her little face and streaking across her rosy, freckled cheek, and seeping into her mother's apron, which was dark grey rather than black from so much washing, and was now taking on a terrible stain, Brigid Kennedy was prompted to action. She lunged for her damp dusting cloth and held it against the wound, yelling to whomever would hear it first: 'Fetch my sewing basket!'

'No! Mum, no! You're not going to sew up my head!' cried Nell.

'Don't be ridiculous, girl. I only want a piece of clean cloth,' her mother roused at her and yelled again down the hall: 'Fetch my sewing basket!'

In all the ruckus and fuss, neither Brigid nor Nell, nor any brother who'd run in off the street after her noticed that Lucky Pete had left the kitchen. Away from the clatter of boots and shoving of elbows and knees and Nell's determination to yell and curse so that she wouldn't cry, little Pete stole away, pinching a box of matches from beside the range as he went.

At not quite four years old and rather coddled, Pete was still a baby in some of the things he did, but he was also too old to be at home alone with only his mum all day, even if it meant he was the plumpest little boy that ever was. He was often bored, and now he was resentful: his biggest brothers, who'd always spoiled him the most, were gone; he'd also just been told by his mother only a matter of an hour ago that he would not be going to school next year but the year after. This last seemed the worse injustice to him. How could it be that he would have to wait so long to go to school? The school was even called Saint Peter's. It was *his* school. It wasn't fair! And now Nell had come home in some kind of trouble again. Nell was always coming home in some kind of trouble, and Pete was getting fearfully jealous about that, too.

Why he did what he did next, though, no-one can explain. Sometimes little ones just do the strangest things, perhaps at the bidding of angels or imps – whichever, it's certain we'll never understand the reason.

Why Pete took that box of matches upstairs to his mother's room and, getting his small self comfortable on her big, high bed, began striking those matches one by one is a mystery for the ages.

As he struck the matches, he looked over at his little cot across from the end of the bed, where he still slept, with his ted and his clown doll, and he didn't want to be a baby anymore.

He wanted to be a big boy; he wanted attention.

He would get the latter soon enough, for he very quickly set his mother's bed on fire.

At first, there were no flames, only a little circle of smouldering linen and curly white smoke floating up from the bed as the fire spread downwards through to the mattress. And then *whoosh* the flames shot up from the coir.

And Pete went running back down the stairs, screaming and waving his fat little arms: 'Mum! Mummy! There's fie on the bed! Fie on the bed!

There's a fie on your big bed!'

Little Pete, being still so little, had not yet mastered his r's. For him, red was still wed, and right was wight – and fire was fie.

His mother, who was now bandaging Nell's poor head, turned to him and told him wearily: 'Well, go and shoo it off.'

She had thought, of course, that he had said there was a fly on her bed. If the truth of her heart be told, she was becoming fairly bored with Pete, too. Sweet as he was, the unbroken company of an almost four-year-old, day in, day out, can test any mother's patience. So many questions, so many complaints, so many desires to toss your beloved child out the nearest window.

'No – Mummy!' he wailed like a banshee. 'A *FIE*. THERE'S A *FIE* ON THE BED!'

At which his mother finally heard him, and then she smelt the evidence of it even as she could barely believe it. And then she blasphemed: 'Oh my God!'

Brigid Kennedy ran then for her life, for the lives of every child in the house and indeed for every life on their side of the street – for if her own terrace house were to go up, it would cause an inferno to race right down the whole line.

By the time she reached the room, bounding up

the stairs two by two, it was full of smoke, and the flames were crackling, flickering, tongues of orange and gold licking up towards the ceiling.

She fought her way through the choking air for the balcony doors that overlooked the street and wrenched them open, as terror and wonder fuelled her nerve to do what she knew she must do next.

The only thing she could do.

Now, Brigid Kennedy was no delicate flower. Even when she'd been a girl, she'd never been small and spry like Nell. Brigid was a broad-shouldered and sturdy woman and, with all the strength of her body and her will combined, she picked up that mattress and, without it touching floor, or wall or curtain, she hoped to throw it out of those balcony doors and into the street.

It was four o'clock in the afternoon, and Crown Street was packed with carts going both ways: fruit and vegetables heading south, up from Paddy's at the Haymarket for next day's selling in all the cheaper grocers, and fruit and vegetables heading in from the countryside, from the Alexandria railhead, for selling at Paddy's tomorrow. There were dogs barking, children playing on the footpaths, a man on a bicycle weaving his way, and Mrs Upton carrying her basket from the shops. It all swirled round and down and round for Brigid Kennedy as she sought what to do with the flaming mattress in her arms.

For the barest of moments she rested the mattress on the edge of the balcony rail; for the barest of seconds she might have considered dropping it on Mrs Upton's head, but she didn't. She shouted out so that the furthest reaches of heaven and hell would hear her: 'Look out! Fire! Look out!' And with all her might she heaved that burning mattress over the rail and hurled it so that it hit nothing and no-one but the footpath below the balcony.

The man on the bicycle stopped at the sound of that great lump of a thing hitting the ground, but he was the only one on the busy street who noticed that anything out of the ordinary had occurred.

Apart from Mrs Upton. She had seen this drama unfold from the moment the mattress appeared teetering on the edge of the balcony. She saw the flames reaching towards the awning of the roof of number 654; she saw the strength with which Mrs Kennedy steered the unwieldy heap of coir so that any tragedy was averted. She saw the selflessness of her neighbour; she saw the power of unthinking, ordinary courage. It was as if Mrs Upton had stuck her head out of her own house and looked up at the blueness of the sunny sky for the first time in her life. She saw what might have happened otherwise: the flames raging through every stick of Crown Street right down to Saint Peter's church, her little Johnny consumed in the blaze. She'd have crossed herself, had she been a Catholic.

As it was, the whispers, privy to privy, spoke only of deliverance, and no-one said too much of a bad word ever about Mrs Kennedy after that. They would not have dared.

Brigid herself had little time to consider it. Pete was at the door of the bedroom now, standing there sobbing: 'Mummy! Mummy! I'm sorry!'

Her Lucky Pete, her little Peter Daniel. His fat little cheeks so red and raw and sore with grief and shame. Her heart was still thumping from the exertion and excitement just past, and when she grabbed up her boy now and crushed him to that heart, she felt the force of all it was to be alive: his fear and his love thumping against her own.

She said: 'Shush now, Petey bub, it's all right.'

He only sobbed, on and on. He was only almost four after all, but although he couldn't tell his mother in words to make it plain, he knew what a terrible, frightening thing he'd done.

And she continued to hold him to her breast; she sat with him in her room on the edge of the frame of the bed till he ran out of sobs and she ran out of disbelief at what she had just done, too, and when he was quiet and calming she said to him: 'Oh my Pete, don't you worry, things could have been worse.'

Little Lucky Pete looked up at his mother from inside her arms. He looked at her with his great big blue eyes, and he reached out his hand and lightly touched her cheek, in that way we all do when we're testing that our miracles are real, and he asked his mother, wondering at the word and the world: 'Worse? What's worse?'

Brigid Kennedy smiled down at her son, and she answered him: 'Well, at least you're not our Nell.'

'Nellie hurt her head,' the little boy said with all his remorse, and his chin began to tremble again that he'd ever had a bad thought for his sister, who was still downstairs in the kitchen, holding the bandage to her head and, like her brothers there with her, none the wiser as to all that had gone on upstairs just now.

'Never mind our Nell.' Pete's mother squeezed him tight. 'Don't you remember the story of the little milkmaid, little Nell of Ballymacyarn?'

The little boy turned in her arms, in her smile: he knew the story. It was Mum's best story ever. He always laughed until his belly hurt when he heard it.

She nodded: 'You remember – our Nell with them skinny legs she's got?'

He nodded back at her, tears forgotten, waiting for her to begin, one of her tales from before he was born, a tale from where he came from.

But she didn't begin now as he had remembered she always did; she said to him over a sigh, closing her eyes: 'Worse, my lad? We all had to leave Ireland because of what Nell did.'

And that was at least half true.

THE LITTLE
MILKMAID

Ellen Mary Kennedy – otherwise known as Nell, Nellie, Hell's Nell, or Stick Legs – was born on New Year's Day, squawking into the dawn of 1906, so loud she brought a ton of snow crashing from the roof. She'd come early, in every way, and so was skinny as a rake from that very first minute of her life. No matter what her mother Brigid fed her, it never stuck to her bones.

And when Nell was small, there was always plenty to eat, even if there weren't too many coins in any pockets. Her family lived in Ballymacyarn, a small village seven miles to the south-west of Tralee towards Dingle and had done ever since anyone could remember. The village sat on a hillside at the foot of the Slieve Mish Mountains, as green as

Erin could ever be, and rolled towards a rocky cliff-top that overlooked the grey Atlantic. There, the Kennedys had three milking cows, never less than twenty-three chickens, and an old stag-pig called Stanley, who'd come to them for his retirement. They ate mackerel three times a week, straight from the sea. They grew potatoes and parsnips and spinach – and carrots all summer, too.

They owned their little plot of land, the Kennedys. It was bought in 1903, by Nell's dad, who was the village blacksmith. He, like many others in the county, took advantage of new laws that had just come in to enable ordinary workingmen to own their own little bit of what their families had dug and ploughed for centuries, since before the English Earls of Desmond took it all up for themselves in 1703, stealing it from the Kings O'Brien. It wasn't worth much. In fact, the minute Dan Kennedy put the money down for it, it was worth quite a lot less, but at least it was theirs. Unfortunately, though, with twelve sons born ahead of Nell, the land was always going to be too small to hand on to them. The sons would need other means of providing for themselves and their future families, and much discussion was had about sending them across to Dublin for work in the factories there, seeing if the sons could be got into trades. But Dublin was expensive, and a risk with too many unknowns: Daniel and Brigid Kennedy didn't want their sons to travel so far away. They'd heard too many stories of boys getting into terrible strife there in Dublin. It was a dilemma.

The eldest of the boys, Dan, was sent only as far as Tralee when he turned sixteen, and for a while the arrangement seemed the ideal thing. Dan could walk the seven miles in to work there on the shipping canal and be home in time for tea – or nearly every day, except for midsummer when the days were long. Gradually, though, as the shipping moved from Tralee canal further round the bay to the new docks at Fenit Harbour, the work began to dry up. By the time his brothers were ready to follow young Dan into Tralee, there were hardly any jobs to be had at all. Their mother and father wondered if they should move the family round to Fenit village, but Fenit already had three blacksmiths, ticketed smiths, working on the wharves – they didn't need another, one who didn't have any formal schooling in his trade, and besides, Fenit was too far away for them to keep their little farm going. They would have had to break up the family somehow, and they just couldn't see their way to doing that. They thought about moving into Tralee itself, so that then the boys could work at Fenit *or* on the canal – Tralee was a county town of near ten thousand, so surely something would come up for them there. But what if it didn't? What if they sold their plot and ended up with nothing and no jobs? The dilemma deepened.

Brigid and Daniel Kennedy decided there and then to pray not to have any more children – thirteen of them was blessing enough, if they didn't think about the reputation of that number too much – but apart from that, they didn't know what to do, except for continuing to enjoy the oversupply of farm labour they increasingly had on their plot. The boys competed with each other as to who could grow the fattest parsnip, or the reddest carrot, and they'd spend hours trying to coax Stanley the old stag-pig into saying hello, which occasionally he did in his grunty way, but apart from that, not much else went on in Ballymacyarn – not for years.

Nell was five, just about five and a half, when Dan came home from Tralee one day, at almost twenty-one years of age, and he told his parents: 'Mam, Da – this is no good. I can't keep going on like this, looking for work that isn't there. My life is passing me by.'

Poor young Dan was in a state of depression about it. He wasn't even in love with any girl to distract him – there were no girls in Ballymacyarn to be distracted by. Year after year, families were moving off their farms and into the towns and the cities; year after year it became more and more difficult for a lad with too little education to get anywhere at all. In fact, it was fairly impossible. The Kennedys knew they would have to do something for their boys, all of them – they would have to make a move sooner or later – but they just couldn't decide when or how. They didn't want to decide – they didn't want to leave their beautiful home.

Why would they? It was paradise on earth in so very many ways. This land gave them so much of all anyone ever needs in nourishment and in beauty. The hill that rose up above the village from behind that gave protection from the gales and trapped the sun upon their fields; in summer the whole of the rise blushed all over with the rainbow splashes of a million wildflowers, and for those few sparkling months of the year, even the Atlantic Ocean would turn on a show: with the brightening of the sky it changed to a deep sapphire blue, and the only grey thing in it would be the whales travelling north on their holidays.

Nell loved to see those whales making their way along the Kerry coast. At first sight of them, she would stop whatever it was she was doing and she would run harum-scarum through the fields and up to the very edge of the cliff, standing on her tiptoes to see them go by. They were called humpback whales in English, and she thought that was an ugly name to give such wonderful creatures. Once, when she saw one of them jump right up out of the sea, she knew she had witnessed the power of God and the love of God in one. *Míol mór*, they were called in Irish, all of the whales. She loved it when her mother spoke that language, but she didn't speak it very often; you didn't want people thinking you were a backwards cottier whose family had made it through the Great Famine by falling down a well and eating frogs, even if that's what you were, so reckoned her mum. Nell reckoned Irish was prettier in every way; she thought their cottage was the prettiest in the village, too.

She'd look back at their place from the cliff-top, the walls of the house bright white against the green hill no matter the weather. Even on the darkest, greyest day, their house was jolly, with the window-sills and the front door all painted red inside the white. All the other houses were just plain stone.

'And where do you think you're going, little Miss Kennedy?' These were words she hated more than any other, for they came from Mrs O'Neill, whose vegetable plot ran beside her own family's. Mrs O'Neill would always grab Nell up under the arm as she said those words, too. She'd reckoned Mrs O'Neill was a witch, because she never saw her coming for her, either. Nell never meant to trespass on her field, but especially with there being no hedgerow between the plots here, she'd just forget where she was sometimes, when she was running, with her head full of wonders and dreams. She had a different engine in her from most others, did Nell: her thoughts would always be running full steam and her stomach would always be churning with some kind of excitement, over and over, round and round, like the way ducks' legs go under water: all the action is happening beneath the surface; but above it you wouldn't know all the effort she was making. When Mrs O'Neill would stop her, witch-fingers pinching in under her arm, Nell would stop still and stare at her. She would stare and stare, wondering at her stupid question: where did Mrs O'Neill ever think Nell might be going? To the moon? She would wriggle in the witch's grip and tell her: 'Let me go!' And with her arms so skinny and her legs so springy and spry, she would always break free and run home.

'That daughter of yours has been tearing up my patch again,' Mrs O'Neill would be banging on the door for her mother to come out.

It wasn't true. Nell never tore up anything. She hardly weighed more than ten feathers in a paper bag, so her dad would always say. 'She couldn't tear a spider web if she ran through it with a hammer,' her mother would tell Mrs O'Neill at the door.

But this wasn't what Mrs O'Neill was so cross about, not at all. The O'Neills were in the same predicament as the Kennedys – too many sons and not enough land, not enough jobs in the towns to go to, either. The only difference was, Mrs O'Neill was a widow, and she was bitter about it. Her husband, Liam, had died from an abscess on a rotten tooth four years ago; Dan Kennedy had offered to get the tooth out for him, as, being a blacksmith, he was the one in the village most expert and best equipped at such things, but Liam had refused, fearing the pain, and so had paid that most terrible price. As well, all four of the O'Neill sons were lazy and wouldn't walk into Tralee if you paid them; they wouldn't chop kindling for their mother, either; they would hardly lift a finger to help her bring in her crop; they certainly wouldn't dare milk the cow. So, any chance she got to rail and rant, she'd take it.

And so Brigid Kennedy would try to keep the peace with her: 'Mrs O'Neill, if my daughter has done any damage, she will right it for you. Show me, what has she done?'

Of course Nell had done nothing, and Mrs O'Neill would stamp off muttering: 'You just keep that girl off my field.'

'Don't you worry about that silly old biddy,' her father would take her up on his knee when he'd come in from the forge and she'd jabber all about it at him. 'And don't you repeat what I just said.' He'd wink. He had the bluest eyes of all the Kennedys, her father did – brightest blue as forget-me-nots. He was the tallest, too, and they were all tall, except for Nell. Her dad was skinny like her, though, while all the others were broad and meaty. He was as skinny as ten pieces of string chucked together, but his arms were strong from his work, belting out rings for the cooper, horseshoes for the farrier, and mending old shovelheads and ploughs. Every fair day he was the man to beat at the arm wrestle. He never lost. In fact, he snapped a man's wrist one time, just like a twig, and shame made him pay the poor fellow's doctor bill before it was even asked for.

Like so many men who are physically strong, Dan Kennedy was gentle in his ways, reluctant to start any fights, too, lest he end up finishing them with consequences he didn't intend. He taught all his sons to be the same: if it wasn't worth going to prison for, it wasn't worth arguing about. And, most importantly, never argue with a woman: no matter what you do, no matter what you say, you'll never win.

He never argued with his wife, Brigid, and that wasn't all because she was his one true darling. He knew that a woman scorned could be terrifying, especially with so many cooking implements always so handy about them – any and all sensible Irishmen knew that – and he thought now that the situation with Mrs O'Neill might be starting to get out of hand. He was also, at the very back of his mind, a little bit concerned that Mrs O'Neill might well have been a witch, as he'd never once seen her cross herself when passing the old oak up at the road going towards Dingle, and so he told his little Nell here on his knee: 'You keep away from Mrs O'Neill, keep off her field, my love, and all will be well.'

'But I don't mean to go there,' Nell whined and squirmed off his knee with a stomp to the floor.

'There're lots of things we don't mean to do that can get us in hot water,' he sympathised, but he insisted, patting his daughter's little shoulder with his great coal-dusty hand: 'Try harder not to go on Mrs O'Neill's field, all right?'

'All right, Daddy,' she told her father, but she screwed up her nose in disgust. Why her father wouldn't march over there to the O'Neills' with a pitchfork was a mystery to her. Mrs O'Neill was not just a witch – she was a liar.

The resentment bubbled and brewed in Nell Kennedy's heart; it swirled and churned inside her belly and her brain. She might only have been five and a half years old, but she could hold the grudge of someone twice that age and ten times the size.

She became extra careful at not putting a foot in Mrs O'Neill's field. She would skip and dance and sing her way up the little dirt path between those two vegetable plots that ran out up the front of their houses towards the sea, and she'd do it just to taunt the woman, but only when her mother or her brothers were looking.

'Oo, Ellen Kennedy,' her mother would rouse, but with half a smile curling on her face: 'You will tempt the Devil in with that act. You stop it, girl.'

She didn't. Her dancing got madder and sillier every time she took that path, and she'd do it now just to make her mother laugh.

Mrs O'Neill would peer from her window,

watching the little girl's every step. Mrs O'Neill could hold a grudge for all of Ireland, in her hurt and crumbling heart.

Until one day, finally, Mrs O'Neill got what she was waiting for.

It was the brightest and prettiest midsummer of 1911, and the hillside was awash with all the pinks and lilacs of the wildflowers, little dashes of yellow splashing about there, too, and Nell had gone up behind the fields to fetch a posy of them for her mother's kitchen table. There were rosy trails of bindweed, and clumps of soft violet cuckoo-bells; there were golden buttercups squiggling everywhere as well, and, if you looked very, very carefully, tiny scarlet pimpernels. Nell spent hours up there choosing exactly the right combination of blooms good for picking – she had quite a knack for such artistic things, an eye for colours and shapes that went well together, and such a posy as she was picking now was the one thing her mother was always pleased about her bringing home.

But there was something missing from this posy, Nell thought to herself when she'd got a good handful of flowers in her little fist. She turned it this way and that, and it was certainly a lovely bunch, a tiny tree of pinks and golds and purples; it just needed – she didn't know what.

'Nellie!' That was her mother calling from the back of the house, from where she was working by the chicken shed. It was time for Nell to get back home – the sun was starting on its way down to the west, scattering spangles all across the sea, and Nell was to help her brothers, Frankie and Chris, at the milking. She was only learning at the milking, but she was already good at it, her small hands swift and strong – and she was keen, so she didn't waste any time skipping back down the hill.

When she got near to the bottom, though, she saw a little flicker of something blue in the scraggedy grass behind the O'Neills': forget-me-nots. A little pocket of those sweet sun-centred blossoms were swaying softly in the breeze over in the shade cast by the back stone wall of the house. *That's* what was missing from her posy. She couldn't see any face at any window; she couldn't see anyone about at the O'Neills' at all, so, quick as a pixie, she darted for their yard, across the lane and over the stile in the hedgerow that ran at the backs of all the fields. She leapt over a pumpkin patch and round the wood pile, and there they were – her forget-me-nots. She snatched up half a dozen stalks, roots and all, and back she ran.

Heart thumping and lungs bursting, she skittered back into her own rear yard and into her house, to place the posy in her mother's white vase. She smiled to herself, Nell did, as she plucked away roots and trimmed off leaves: she hadn't gone into Mrs O'Neill's patch, not technically, she hadn't gone anywhere near her vegetable rows, and she hadn't even really stolen anything, either. These forget-me-nots were just a bunch of weeds. But she had a little shiver in there, too, as she arranged the flowers in their vase just right: she couldn't believe she'd got away with it.

Because she hadn't. Mrs O'Neill had seen the whole thing from behind the curtain over her kitchen window. She'd seen the little girl take the flowers from almost right under her nose, and even though they might have been more pests in her string beans than anything else to her, Mrs O'Neill considered that they were *her* forget-me-nots, and that this was a felony of the worst order. But Mrs O'Neill didn't march straight up to the Kennedys' door. No. She waited this time. She waited until Mrs Kennedy was finished her work. She watched the other woman at her business: taking a chicken with her hatchet. She certainly wasn't going to pick a bone with Mrs Kennedy while she was armed. She waited until Mrs Kennedy was busy plucking. She knew that Mrs Kennedy enjoyed sitting there in the summer sun of the afternoon, plucking, plucking, contented in the warmth. It would be the perfect time to interrupt her for maximum annoyance – for, oh, Mrs O'Neill was spoiling for a fight.

By this time, Nell was way over the other side of the back of the Kennedys' yard, sitting there on the milking stool and tending to one of the cows; two of the boys – the older twins, Frankie and Chris – were working with her.

Mrs O'Neill didn't knock on the front door as she usually would. She just appeared, like a tortured otherworldly apparition, waving her arms and bawling: 'Thief! Thief! You wretched little thief!'

At which all four Kennedys – Brigid, Frankie, Chris and Nell – looked up from their work. Even the chickens pecking round the yard stopped to look.

Brigid Kennedy stood, a small cloud of feathers about her: 'To what do we owe this pleasure, Mrs O'Neill?'

'Pleasure?' The woman was insane with rage. 'Your daughter stole flowers from my yard.'

They were all still stuck in silence at that, especially Mrs Kennedy, for although she'd surely scold and spank her daughter if this were true, the rage in

Mrs O'Neill's eyes did not seem quite warranted in the situation.

After some moments of the two women staring at each other, one insane, one querying, Mrs Kennedy said: 'Well, all right, now, Mrs O'Neill. Let's see if we can't sort this out. Ellen Mary!' she called and moved towards her daughter, shouting out her whole name to show that the girl was in a big fat pot of hot water.

But only Frankie and Chris stood up from their milking, as if she might have shouted Francis-Joseph-Christopher-Luke, as she often did. Nell stayed sitting right where she was, on her milking stool. Her little heart was banging again, and her belly was churning in seventeen different directions, but she kept on at the milking, as if she didn't hear. Maggie the brown cow's teats were the easiest of all, and she loved milking her. She wasn't stopping for anything. She listened only to the ping and splosh of the streams of milk hitting the side of her bucket. How she loved milking. She loved the smell; she imagined it was the smell of crushed up, munched up wildflowers.

There was now a small but fierce war broken out behind her, though.

'Forget-me-nots?' her mother was shrieking,

feathers now flying off her apron as she threw her arms up in the air. 'You'll get a policeman round for this, will you? Well, go on then, we could all do with a laugh!'

'You'll be laughing round the other side of your face if you're not careful,' Mrs O'Neill threatened back, and it was a menacing threat of violence.

Nell wasn't sure what that expression meant – she didn't know how anyone could laugh out of the other side of their face, or if you could have any more than one side to your face at all. She only knew that it was nasty – that Mrs O'Neill was the nastiest witch that ever was. And so young Nell did the only thing she could do, in the circumstances.

As the women argued and chickens flapped and squawked all around them, little Nell angled Maggie's teat upwards from the bucket in her hot little hand, and she squeezed and pulled that teat with all her care – and squirted Mrs O'Neill smack bang in the middle of her fat red face. In fact, she got her right up the left nostril with a steaming jet of milk.

Well, didn't Frankie and Chris fall down laughing at that.

Unfortunately, so did their mother.

A full-blown feud broke out now between the

families. The O'Neill boys, who never got off their lumpy backsides, surely got off them now. For pride is most often the most compelling and dangerous of things. No fists were thrown, but to the Kennedys' horror, Stanley the stag-pig was found prematurely expired in his stall one dawn; and to the O'Neills' great alarm, their haystack spontaneously combusted the following night.

Even still, the police were got down from Tralee thrice on matters of more nonsense such as this before Brigid and Daniel Kennedy could bring themselves to agree: to say goodbye to Ballymacyarn. To find some other place to be.

MAKING WAVES

'Tell me what happened when you all went on the ship,' I ask Grandma's sad smile, trying again to get her to tell me one of her stories, to take us away, but she only looks away, out through the blinds. She's looking towards town from the kitchen window. I don't think she's really looking at anything, though.

I look down at my skirt: it's green, with tiny white polka dots, and round the hem there are two rows of purple zigzag ribbon – rick rack, it's called, and it's wavy, like the sea. I remember asking Granddad, when Grandma finished it, ages ago, how she got the ribbon to stick on the skirt, because I couldn't see any stitches in it, and Granddad winked at me and said: 'Magic.'

Grandma says now: 'What did you say?'

I ask her again: 'Tell me about the time you all

came on the ship, to Australia.'

It's a story she's usually happy to tell, with Mum groaning, 'Oh, not that one again.'

But Grandma says, 'Not today, Bridge love.'

I don't think she really heard me anyway.

Her cigarette smoke swirls between the slats of the blinds and all along the window.

When I look down again, the purple zigzag waves on my skirt look like the picture of the sea that Sister Regina drew on the blackboard in her history lesson just before we broke up for the holidays. She drew some sailing ships above the waves and told us all that Australia was stolen from the Aboriginals by the British Empire in colonial times. She got into trouble for that – someone made a complaint. Granddad shook his head at the fuss and said, 'That poor, sweet sister is only a child herself – and she's right.'

I wish I could tell Grandma that I miss him, too.

But I know my missing him is nothing to talk about. It's just a drop in her ocean. I eat the rest of my burnt circle toast instead and then I go and sit on the sofa, to leave her to look out the window in peace. I remember the story of how she came to Australia. I can tell it to myself, today.

ALL AT SEA

Still with half a hope of finding a miracle that might allow them to stay, Dan Kennedy went round to Father Maloney, their village priest, to see what he had to say. Now, Father Maloney was not unlike Stanley the stag-pig had lately been, in that he was fairly much on retirement, only he was, on this occasion, slightly more alive.

'Have you considered Australia?' the old priest asked him straight out over a whiskey, in his little presbytery out the back of the church yard.

And Dan Kennedy shook his head: 'No, Father, I haven't.'

It was an odd question, so Dan thought. Why should he have considered going to Australia, when he thought Dublin was too far away at a hundred and seventy miles? He knew Australia was a long way distant. He knew of whole families that had gone there, whole chunks of Ireland removed during the famine in his grandparents' day, and all the hard years after, never to return. He heard stories of those who had died starving and filthy on the long journey, too. But he didn't know just how far away it was.

So he asked the priest: 'How far is it to Australia then?'

'Twelve thousand miles, thereabouts,' said the priest.

'Twelve what?' Dan almost spluttered his mouthful of whiskey all over the priest. He couldn't imagine such a distance. Limerick, to him, was the furthest he'd ever been known to travel anywhere, eighty miles, and that was only once, to sow a wild oat before marrying – and there he'd met Brigid Sheady from Shannon instead, who was only there farewelling her brothers bound for Canada. His own brothers, all younger, were in America, in Philadelphia and Pittsburgh – five of them, left one by one across the 1890s, his three sisters all marrying men who did the same, and he'd never heard from any of them again, apart from a brief letter here or there, which Brigid had to read for him. It was something he didn't like thinking about much less discussing – this heartbreak of illiteracy and distance. Well, that's that done for a consideration, he thought. Australia might as well be on the bottom of the sea then. He couldn't take his family there. If they were going to leave Ireland, maybe they'd just have to go to America – *if* they could get in. It was getting harder and harder to settle over there, he'd heard. It was getting harder and harder to see his way clear. Only one thing was certain: they weren't going to Dublin – that city full of trouble and sin.

'A man can make something of himself there, in Australia,' Father Maloney went on regardless. 'The sun shines ceaselessly, the trade unions are strong, and there are jobs aplenty as the government has lately thrown every black man and Chinaman out of work.' He said that last as if God might approve, and added: 'Do the work no Englishman can lower himself to do and you'll rise above them. Wages for a dustman are highest across the Empire. Your boys will have the best opportunity there.'

'But is it a safe place, free of trouble? A moral place?' Dan Kennedy asked, thinking ceaseless sunshine, high wages and jobs aplenty was sounding a bit too good to be true.

And yet the priest told him, 'Oh yes,' sitting back in his chair, a little bit the worse for drink but no less convincing for it. 'Cardinal Moran has transformed Sydney into the Irishman's Paradise – there's a church on every second corner, and a pub in between. It'll be the best thing you've ever done. My nephew over in Tralee, he's with the immigration office at Customs House – he'll get all the papers done for you.'

And for a not insignificant fee that's just what he would do, too.

Brigid sighed when her husband came home and told her of the idea. 'Well, my darling,' she said, for want of having this over with, 'let's make it done then. You know I'll go anywhere with you, and if we're going to go anywhere, if we're going to take such a risk, then why not take the biggest risk, take the biggest distance of all?'

Dan nodded, tired of thinking about it, too: 'Yes. Why not?' Who was he to doubt the word of a priest anyway?

'We're going to Australia!' All the Kennedy boys jumped around the kitchen, hooting and hooraying, especially young Dan – he hooted and hoorayed with relief. Anything had to be better than staying stuck here in backward, nowhere and nothing Ballymacyarn.

Little Nell wasn't so sure.

'But I don't want to go to Austra-whatever-it-is. I want to stay here,' she said, but her small voice of trepidation could not be heard that day.

Nor on the day they left Ballymacyarn, their papers in order, their little farm sold, the forge, too, their tickets booked on the train that would take them to the ship that would take them to Plymouth, so that they could meet another ship that would then take them – into the black of endless night, Nell feared, although she didn't quite know why beyond the not wanting to leave all that she had ever known, never mind the boggling terror the train whistle brought her as they pulled away across the Kerry countryside bound for Killarney, bound for Cork.

Her father was quietly fearful himself as he held her little hand up the ramp of the first boat, a rusting mail packet going out of Cork Harbour; he could barely believe that he'd just spent almost all of their earthly worth on their fares and accommodations and fees – £243 in all – and that he was about to do something he never dreamed he ever would do: set foot in England. Dan Kennedy would rather have gone via Canada, or New York, straight across the Atlantic – he'd rather have gone via Iceland in a tiny curach with all his children piled up on his head and

Brigid on his knee – if he could avoid setting foot in England by doing so, but it couldn't be arranged.

As they left the Irish coast from the mouth of the Lee, Dan Kennedy held his small daughter's hand tighter for seeing his green country disappear into the grey of the mist and the sea for the last time. There was no question of ever coming back; it was not in the realms of his imagination, nor practical reality, that he would ever raise the fare again to return. He would never again have a farm to sell – nor a Father Maloney to arrange for the church to purchase it at such a fair price as he'd got, or so he'd been assured. That his family had held on to that little patch of Ballymacyarn through famine that stole a million lives, and before that through generations of penury by taxes and rents charged by generations of lords who ruled over them, only for him to leave now in this whispering, dragging defeat smashed him to pieces inside. He felt so near to crying, his wife knew not to say a word to him as he gazed out across the Celtic Sea. Instead, Brigid allowed a fight to break out among Frank, Chris and Dom over their positions at the ship's rail, which prompted the older boys to devise a distraction by applying their lips and great lungfuls of breath to their palms for a grand chorus of farting in farewell to Erin, which could not fail to make their father smile in gratitude for all he truly owned.

And when they arrived in Plymouth, twenty-two freezing February hours later, Dan Kennedy could almost have wept for seeing the vessel that would take them onwards: the Orient Steam Navigation Company's RMS *Oberon* was no coffin ship of old: it was sturdy and clean and new, with four bunks in each of their two cabin rooms, a great big dining hall and plenty of decent food. They would survive the journey.

Although little Nell remained unsure.

The potatoes were lumpy and floury, the stews were thin and the bread was always stale. Nell would never have made so much as a squeak of complaint at such things – she'd learned too well, even at the age of only lately turned six, that whining about food not being to your liking was a mortal sin. She kept her concern shut up tight behind her big blue, worried eyes, but worry indeed she did. She was sure that it was the potatoes' fault her mother was sick the whole way on the ship so far – after all, they made Nell herself gag just about every day. But of course Nell couldn't have known the real reason her mother was unwell: it wasn't the potatoes; it wasn't even the swaying and rolling of the sea. It was another baby coming, one not even her mother yet knew about.

Whatever the cause might have been, to see her mother so poorly all the time, was evidence to Nell of the wrongness of the world opening up around and around her as the weeks unfurled. With each new glimpse of its wideness and strangeness – through Gibraltar, Toulon, Naples, Port Said, Suez, Colombo – with every wild sight and odd smell, Nell's fears drove deeper. They churned and tumbled inside her, in a way she'd never known churning before. Her worries whirred in time with the ship's engine and buzzed amid the clattering clamour of foreign tongues. She wasn't sure where it occurred – it could have been Egypt or Ceylon – but a man with skin as rusty-brown as hot, steaming chicory and a turban as blue as the sky, bent down to her and, smiling a half-toothless smile, he touched her on the head and scared her almost half to death. She was with her brother Dan, and she hid straight behind his leg. Nell was not a hider behind legs, though. She was a girl who, despite her smallness, would always put herself up the front of the line. What was wrong with her?

'Don't worry,' said Dan, always the gentlest of her brothers. 'You're as strange to him as he is to you – he only likes your mad red hair.'

'Well, I don't like him,' Nell said, and shrank further away. She didn't mean to say such an awful thing – how can anyone not like or like a stranger? It was strangeness she didn't like, in all its many colours, a small and silent burden of dismay she'd carry like a pebble from now on.

'Oh my dear God,' her mother crossed herself when they finally found Australia. She was reading a newspaper, in a place called Fremantle, with still several days' sailing to go, and she'd just learned from the page she was reading that the *Titanic* had sunk.

'What's the *Titanic*?' Nell scrambled to her mother's side, searching the sea of newspaper words for sense, although she couldn't yet read much herself.

'A big ship,' her mother said, more to her father than to her. 'The biggest passenger ship in the world. She's hit an iceberg – in the Atlantic. Fifteen hundred lost – oh, those poor souls!' Her mother did something else then that Nell had never seen her do before: she allowed her eyes to well with tears and even let one of them fall down her cheek.

Of course, Nell couldn't have known that this tear, like all her mother's disconcerting poorliness along this voyage, was only another sign of the baby who was on his way. No, to Nell, this was all more proof that whatever this journey was that her parents had embarked upon, it was the worst thing that could have happened.

And after thinking about it for quite some time now, Nell realised that there was only one person in all of her family that could be blamed for what had befallen the Kennedys: and that was her small but wicked self. It was Nell's fault that they'd had to sell up and leave their farm; it was Nell's fault that Stanley the stag-pig was killed in his stall with his blood all running out into the mud along the edge of the stone path there and reaching towards the back step; it was her fault that they were all here now, tossed on the black sea, bound soon, surely, to hit a subtropical iceberg and plunge to the fathom-less depths – just like the *Titanic*. If only she hadn't teased and taunted Mrs O'Neill, and squirted her with Maggie's milk.

So, somewhere between Adelaide and Melbourne, and wedged as she was between two of her brothers, Tom and Jack, at the foot of her mother's bunk, Jack, who was seven, whispered out in the night, half in annoyance and half in concern: 'Nellie's crying.'

'What's got you, girl?' her mother was quick to sit

up and hold her daughter to her as she sobbed, and quick mostly to try to prevent the other four boys in the bunk above from waking up at the sound.

But Nell had dwelt on this so long, she fairly wailed it out to wake all of steerage up.

'Nell, you silly girl,' her mother said when her daughter had finished blubbering and carrying on. 'You might be trouble, but you're our trouble, and a slim package of it at that. We are blessed to have you in our hearts – never doubt that. But you didn't cause us to come on this ship. It is arrogance to think such a thing – and arrogance is a sin. Be quiet now and go back to sleep.'

Nell did as she was told, she quietened her tears and snuggled back down, but despite her mother's reassuring warning of hellfire if she didn't stop thinking everything was her fault, it had seeped into her soul as some kind of knowledge now, and her little pebble of dismay at strangeness became tight wound with threads of guilt.

Small pebbles wound with thread or not are easily put away in pockets or tied in the end of your handkerchief, though, aren't they, like a rosary bead or a Saint Christopher medal slipped off its chain, and such was Nell's, so that in the photograph that was taken of the Kennedys by a curious immigration officer when they disembarked in Sydney, you couldn't tell she carried a pebble at all.

Her smile was the sunshine itself that glimmering, shimmering afternoon they arrived at Circular Quay. It was a perfect day of warm, bright light and cool, sweet breezes. Seagulls swirled; tram-bells dinged; there was a welcoming smell of fish and chips wrapped in newspaper, and although Nell has never known any fish and chips but those her mother had cooked for her, it smelled something like home. It wasn't near as green, but it was vastly more blue – so blue, if the sky could shout out and throw its hat in the air, it would. It was the twenty-ninth of April, 1912, or perhaps it was the thirtieth – no-one could ever precisely remember the date – but they were here, somewhere, at last.

OUT OF THE BLUE

The sky isn't very blue today: it's too hot to be bothered. I've been staring out the window at it, with Grandma – not the same kitchen window as hers but the one along, above the sofa. I'm kneeling on the seat cushions, and even that doesn't make her look at me. Normally, she would say, 'Sit round properly or you'll wear a hole.'

I sit round anyway, and when I do I stare straight into the bright-blue eye of one of the peacock feathers in the vase that sits on the telephone table just beside Grandma's bedroom door. The vase has an African lady dancing on it, and the flowers in it are pretend ones: golden wattle sprays, Grandma's happy flowers, she always says, but she likes the plastic ones so they don't make a mess everywhere with their pollen and make her sneeze. The peacock feathers are real, though. They stand tall in the vase, three bright-blue eyes above the wattle, their floaty edges always dancing, like the lady, even when there is no breeze. Granddad bought them for her: a man was selling them at Central station one time, where he changes trains for Fairfield, on the Cumberland Line, or so he used to, on his way to work. I don't know exactly when he got the peacock feathers, but I wish I did know. I wish I could remember everything.

Maybe I should go over to the sink and clean up our lunch things, but I don't want to make any clanky noise to interrupt whatever Grandma is thinking. She must be thinking something, staring out at the faded, smudgy sky the way she is. She's probably thinking about him.

I sneak over to the radiogram, at the other end of the sofa, where I've left my book. It's just an old school book that I'm scribbling in the back of, to use up the pages. I'll write a story of my own now. I'll write one for Grandma and Granddad.

HER ONE TRUE
DARLING

Nell Kennedy fell in love with Stevie O'Halligan
in the playground at St Peter's School sometime
near the beginning of September 1913. She was
seven and three-quarter years old; he was just turned
ten, and he was playing donkey-league with all the
other boys. It was always a rough game, where they'd
organise themselves into two teams, each boy taking
another onto his back and then the teams would run
altogether at each other in a clash of boots and heads.
Normally, Nell didn't watch them – she saw enough of
all that sort of thing in her own house, especially now
her mother was always busy with the baby. But this
day, her eye was caught by the snowy hair of this new
boy, Stevie. He was tall and strong and he just about
danced as he ran, darting through the pack of boots

and heads, with fat Andy Collins on his back. Her heart was caught when this Stevie boy stopped still amid the scrum to pick up one who had fallen down and grazed his knee. The way Stevie O'Halligan placed his hand on the other boy's shoulder to see that he was all right made Nell know that this was the boy she would marry one day. Someone brave and gentle, just like her dad.

But within the month, both had vanished. Her dad didn't come home one day, nor ever again. It wasn't the done thing for a child so young as Nell to attend a burial or a funeral mass in those days, of course, so Nell couldn't ever quite make sense of it. She didn't quite believe her dad was gone. Run over by a cart going too fast downhill on its way to Paddy's? Witches' fingers of chicory root smashed all over the street? Couldn't they find her dad under the sacks that toppled from the cart? What did the witches do with him? She dreamed it and dreamed it, but could never find him herself. Then Stevie, it soon became apparent, had gone, too. She summoned up the courage to ask the teacher, Sister Gregory, if Stevie had died as well, but the sister told her kindly: 'No, lass, Steven has only gone back to his home. He lives in the countryside. He was only visiting for a time.' Still, Nell looked for him in the playground every day, just as she listened for her father's footfall to come down the hall every evening.

Life went on: her mother chasing baby Pete around and daily mourning the loss of her garden at Ballymacyarn, for she had no garden here in Surry Hills to feed her family. For all the sunshine and for all the enormous quantities of horse manure throughout the streets, the quality of vegetables for sale in this city was a travesty – as was their extortionate price. The meat was always tough and on the turn; sausages tasted of sawdust; the tripe was leathery. But Nell never once complained; she overheard her eldest brother Danny crying alone in the lane one night when she crept out to the privy, a sound that made her promise never to complain even in her thoughts. When she was sitting out on the back step one afternoon, pushing her fist into her belly to stop it churning around nothing, to push the hunger pain from her with another, her brother Pat sat down beside her and gave her the smoke he'd just rolled: 'Here,' he said. 'It helps.'

It did in a strange way: the burning down her throat was another pain keeping the hunger at bay, while the dizzy spell it gave her made her laugh; and that made Pat laugh, too. Even Danny laughed at the sight of his tiny sister having a puff. She could also have as many cigarettes as she liked, for while her brothers had such trouble getting work that would pay the rent, they were regularly enough called upon by a fellow from Customs House to help with the unloading and concealment of contraband tobacco and opium come in on ships here and there from Manila. Nell was not aware of any of these illicit goings-on, of course, nor that this relationship between the authorities and the Kennedy boys would ultimately help them in setting up their little betting shop round the corner in Elizabeth Lane. All she knew was that, one day soon, they were moving on again.

It was only up the hill to the top of Crown Street, and it didn't have garden enough for anything but a handful of tomatoes and beans, but it was big and she even had her own room – sort of. It was an alcove beside her mother's bed where a wardrobe was supposed to go, and it was diagonally opposite Pete's cot, too, but it felt like her very own room. Her brothers had made her a special bed from an old door stacked up on bricks to fit the space, all draped with a curtain of lavender velvet Mick had got just for her – a whole bolt of the stuff, which had by some trick of fate fallen off the back of a cart.

Life went on: a war began in Europe, lighting up war with the Uptons and the Boyles down the road, her three eldest brothers then disappeared in uniform, and Pete nearly burned down the house. Pete – that Lucky little Pete – was so annoying, he could get away with murder. Somewhere in her heart, she knew that her mother clung to that last little boy for all that she'd lost when her husband died, and all the fearfulness she felt for her boys gone abroad, but Nell harboured a little streak of hatred for him nevertheless. Pete had almost incinerated her lavender curtain, but there were a thousand more reasons to hate him than that: the way their mother would always give him the biggest share of apple peelings, or the bone of her chop to suck, or the last stick of rhubarb sprinkled with sugar – it all drove Nell quietly insane. No wonder Pete couldn't talk properly, she'd grumble to herself – their mother was always shoving food in his mouth, or pinching his fat little cheeks. Nell couldn't get five minutes of her mother's attention even if Johnny Upton tried to kill her in the street.

Nell took every opportunity to keep out of the house, whenever her mother didn't need her. She'd roam all the way along Cleveland Street and across to Centennial Park, sometimes with her brothers

Tommy or Jack, and once or twice with Eileen Tighe, her friend from school who lived halfway there on South Dowling Street, but mostly she'd go alone, just because she liked to be alone, walking, walking, going to the park. She loved those long hours of freedom on a Saturday afternoon or long summer evening and, once inside the park, she'd take off her shoes to feel the cool of the clover beneath her bare feet; she'd close her eyes and pretend she was back in Ballymacyarn. Her memories of her home in Ireland were already fading into dreams, but she'd find her longing and her fill of love in the tiny flowers she'd spy on her walks, and it was always worth being bawled out by her mother for being late in just to see them. Tiny lilac stars of onion weed, drifts of even tinier white daisies she'd never know the name of, and graceful little sky-coloured bells that everyone called blueberries, that weren't berries at all but small lilies that grew somehow miraculously out of half-dead seeming clumps of grass. These last were the colour of forget-me-nots; they were the colour of her father's eyes. They weren't neat spots of sky like her Irish forget-me-nots, though; these were raggedy and drooping splotches of blue, but they were her forget-me-nots – here, in this city. She dreamed they were raggedy and drooping from the fairies wearing them out at their midsummer balls. They were very sad and very beautiful all at the same time.

But, oddly enough, her favourite new flower was the strangest, one that was like none from her old home: it was the golden wattle. On the first day of spring each year, now that she was in primary school, her whole class would go out into the countryside to pick great armfuls of these cheerful, bobbling blooms to decorate the church and the schoolrooms for Wattle Day. The so-called countryside wasn't very far out of the city – it was only a patch of scrub a few miles away at Kingsford, just off the tram line, but every time they went there, she'd look out again for Stevie O'Halligan, wondering where in the country he was. Until she started sneezing. With her arms full of wattle, she would sneeze – and sneeze, and sneeze a thousand times – so the whole class would be tumbling around laughing, even the Sisters. That was always the best part of the day. That such laughter could burst from so little; that this bush that had only a week or so ago been so dull and grey was now so suddenly shouting with happy colour.

School was Nell's most happy place, though. There was always so much to do and think and dream, that whatever else might have been going on went well by the wayside while she was there. Her teacher was Sister Mary-Bernadette, and Nell was one of her favourites – she was always being picked to read out for the class, or to sing, as Sister Mary-Bernadette said Nell had the music of the south-west in her voice – the south-west of Ireland, that is. The school even had a little library of its own, and Nell could borrow books and take them home, books of bible stories, fables and fairytales – and even an illustrated book of carpentry that Nell was quite taken with for a while.

Her mother wasn't always as enthusiastic about her daughter's schooling, however. Brigid Kennedy was suspicious of anything that went beyond the three r's – especially for a girl. A girl shouldn't be too well educated – only enough to read for her husband as required, but never enough to embarrass him. And when she learned that the Lasallian Brothers at the boys' Superior school wanted to bring classes for Gaeilge into not only that establishment, but for the little ones still with the Sisters of Mercy at Saint Peter's, she was moved to make a protest at the parents' meeting. The language of Ireland might have been romantic for some whose families had left generations ago, but it was a stigma still fresh and sharp for many newer arrivals: it was the language of illiteracy, poverty and prejudice, and Brigid Kennedy would not have her children speaking a word of it. She was straight-backed and adamant with terror at what the failed Easter Rising in Dublin just past would bring them now, too: the Irish rebels had been rounded up and murdered by the British lords, as you would expect – but would that mean bullets rather than bricks through windows in the streets of Surry Hills now? It didn't, but neither did the push for Irish patriotism in the schools go ahead. Still, having picked up tantalising pieces of the argument herself, every day at school little Nell Kennedy waited to hear the music of her Irish language, but she never did again.

Instead, she received a special letter from her brother Pat, from the trenches in France, reminding her to work hard at her lessons, because he was putting money aside to see to it that she would go on to high school at St Anne's. She slept with that letter under her pillow to see to it that all wars would end, and that he would come home, bringing Danny and Mick with him.

A most extraordinary thing occurred before the war did end, though: Stevie O'Halligan reappeared, in the March of 1918. Nell was walking out of the schoolyard, taking the long way round via Marlborough Street past the boys' school, to avoid run-ins with the nasty Prots across the blocks along Crown, when she saw him. She knew him by his snowy hair and the smooth but strapping way he walked. She had to stop herself from calling out, even though she'd never once spoken to him before. She was twelve years old; he was almost fifteen.

Something made him turn around and the sun came out as it had never done. He said, as smooth and strapping as his walk: 'I know you, don't I? Miss Kennedy, isn't it?'

Up until this day, no-one had ever called her 'Miss'. She didn't know which knee to hide behind the other, or how she'd work the look of stupidity off her face now that it was there.

Inside she whirled madder than her mad red hair, she curled and unfurled all at the same time. But, Nell being Nell, all Stevie O'Halligan saw was a girl standing there with her hand on her hip, telling him with some impatience: 'I'm not sure that I can say I know you.'

But she did, oh she did. They already knew each other very well, for Stevie, so smooth and so strapping on the outside, was a storm of nerves on the inside. He couldn't believe he'd just spoken to

Nell Kennedy at all. He'd been watching her walk past the gates of his school every afternoon now for almost a month, since his return to Sydney from the farm at Guyong. He'd asked one of his classmates who she was – as he really, truly thought he knew her. Even if he didn't, she was the prettiest girl he'd ever seen.

He said to her: 'I know you.'

And then he dared to walk her home – bold as that! In broad daylight. As they walked, he did the talking: he told her he was back in Sydney staying with his Aunt Hannah over in Cooper Street, because the Brothers wanted him for a rugby team.

Rugby? She didn't much care why he was here now. She wanted to ask him why he'd come for that tiny speck of time five years ago, though; she wanted to see if the hand of God was at work between them. She wanted to ask Stevie O'Halligan if he and his aunt would like to go on a picnic in Centennial Park but, although it was entirely inappropriate that she should make any such suggestion, she couldn't open her mouth to say anything all.

When he left her to continue on his way home, she didn't hear his cheerio. She couldn't hear anything above the chorus of angels that had just gone off in her head – she couldn't feel the front step under her feet for the wings that carried her.

'What's got into you, girl?' her mother asked her as they sat across the kitchen table from each other, peeling potatoes, having noticed that Nell had left great chunks of skin all over her lot.

'Nothing,' Nell told her mother, but Brigid knew. She saw the little smirk on her daughter's face, the little blush on her cheeks – she knew – and from then on, Nell was not allowed to go traipsing round the neighbourhood without one of her brothers or a girlfriend for company.

'But, Mum – why?' Nell protested a few days later, when she wanted to wander to the park – secretly, via Cooper Street.

And her mother said: 'Do as you are told.'

'But—'

'Do as you're told or get to the Devil.' She said it twice – once in Irish, under her breath.

There was no arguing with Brigid Kennedy after that, and so Stevie O'Halligan walked Nell Kennedy home most afternoons in the company of Eddie or Tom or Jack, or all three, and often Sean and Martin as well, providing a humiliating chorus of 'Hell's Nells has got a sweetheart, hell's bells and ain't he too smart.' So smart, Stevie was, he never responded with anything but a good-natured smile no matter how much he wanted to smash their heads together.

It was a situation that did not alter when the news finally arrived that the war had ended – Frankie and Chris had raced home from the post office with the news so that their mother could get it first. Brigid Kennedy's humour did not improve where the O'Halligan boy was concerned even after she received the news that all three of her own elder boys were safe in London, awaiting a ship home. Brigid would not even meet with Steven's Aunt Hannah to make her acquaintance. Her daughter was not thirteen yet. She was far too young. She didn't want her daughter married at sixteen as she had been, much as she had cherished every moment of her own marriage. Whoever the lad would be for her Nell, he'd have some education past merit certificate – a trade perhaps, or a clerkship – and a good job already under his belt, he'd have money put away for his future family before he'd even thought to take a wife. He would not be a pimply-faced, football-playing bumpkin from the bush. She'd heard, privy to privy, his father was a pig farmer. She thought she might as well send her daughter back to Ballymacyarn when she'd heard that. When she'd heard he was a pig farmer from County Armagh, that settled it – her daughter would not be going with some dark-tempered ruffian from the north.

She wouldn't change her mind, even when Dan and Mick and Pat came home in the winter of 1919, all of them needing a long spell in the fattening paddock of their mother's kitchen, all of them needing the beauty of their little sister and safety of their small world of home to keep the sadness from their eyes for all they'd seen of pointless violence and tragedy in the world abroad. Pat, in particular, was haunted, not only by the ghosts of the battlefield but by ghosts put in his lungs from mustard gas – he would never be quite well again. Not that this marred any Kennedy rejoicing. They ate more and laughed harder against any pain, they tossed Lucky Pete higher, though he now weighed a small ton, and when the news came through that Pat, who had risen to the rank of lieutenant in the army, was now accepted into the University of Sydney to study to be a lawyer, his mother fainted. She'd been standing by the stove making a custard and collapsed to the floor in her wonder and awe. A Kennedy? Going to university? She would never quite believe that had occurred.

But the boys had brought home with them the tail of something wicked: although none of them were sick with it themselves, their ship had brought a deadly load of Spanish flu from Arabia. It ripped and slashed its way through the neighbourhood and killed ten children in one night.

And one of those children was little Lucky Pete. He'd had a sniffle and a sneeze on a Friday afternoon, and he was dead in a boiling fever by the Sunday morning. He was not quite seven.

The bells of Saint Peter's tolled black over Surry Hills.

The shock of it stunned the streets to silence. Even cartwheels seemed to whisper; horses' shoes trod soft. The Uptons and the Boyles brought gifts of food and flowers to Brigid Kennedy's door, in permanent truce. In peace, and love.

Nell's mind was blank to it all, at first. From the moment she heard her mother scream from Pete's bedside, Nell could not form a thought. She made cups of tea for her mother, cups of tea for the priest; she kept her brothers' bellies filled even as she couldn't think to eat herself.

She went to the funeral mass for her little brother – she was old enough for that these days – but she wasn't allowed to go to the burial. It wouldn't do anyone any good for her to see her mother throw herself to the ground as it received her little son.

All the while, though Nell could barely see him, Stevie O'Halligan was there. He held her hand all the way home that day as any other, and at her gate this day, as she felt his hand in hers, Nell began to cry. It would be the very last time she ever really cried, like this, so openly, for shame and grief, for dismay and guilt, holding her pebble to her heart for Pete, for her mother and for herself, and she cried as if she knew this would be the very last time.

Stevie didn't say 'there, there' or 'shush now'. Into her anguish he said the only thing he could think of that was larger than this; he told her with all his heart as she cried: 'I'll always love you, Nell Kennedy.'

She put her pebble in her shoe that moment, that day, and left it there, so that she would feel it wherever she went, every day for the rest of her life.

FOREVER AND
EVER, AMEN

They were married on the sixteenth of March, 1924, the day before Saint Patrick's Day, and all the jolly green bunting through the streets might as well have been for them, they were so happy. Nell was eighteen and Stevie almost twenty-one. He wore a smart suit of silvery grey he'd had made at Blumberg's, the Jewish tailor in Foveaux Street, and she wore a gown and veil of ivory tambour lace she made herself from fabric she'd saved for and had put away for almost two years, love and devotion in every stitch. They were the most beautiful couple that ever lived, as all young newlyweds are.

Even still, Nell's mother had not relented in her attitude towards her one and only son-in-law.

Despite their wait of six years, despite Stevie not going on to play any football as a result of an unfortunate injury to his left knee during a match against Saint Joseph's in his final year of school, despite his getting a position as a junior clerk with the Department of Lands at seventeen and studying bookkeeping at night, despite his insistence that Nell herself go on to business college from high school to get her stenography and typing qualifications, despite his strong body and perfect teeth, despite his unfailingly kind heart, Brigid Kennedy considered Stevie to be merely a pig-farmer's son from Armagh, and therefore not good enough for her daughter. No matter how much all her own sons teased her for her bigotry, she would not relent.

No matter how much Nell tried to show how happy and bright her future was, she could not push open this door to shed even the tiniest crack of light upon her mother's dark opinion. Nell knew that her mother still suffered the heartbreak of losing Peter the way they had. She knew that, for her mother, it was as if the sun would never quite rise again, that joy would never be hers to have or hold. Nevertheless, Brigid's refusal to accept Steven as Nell's husband, to treat him with any regard or warmth, forced a rift to grow between mother and daughter. There were no passionate words spoken, no tantrums or tears, but a cool and sorrowful drifting apart.

'Don't worry, Sis,' Dan told her. 'Ma will give it up when the babies come.'

It was true that Brigid had treated Dan's wife, Maureen, with similar disdain when they were married four years earlier – and Mick's wife, Gwenda, when they married a year after that, and Pat's wife, Marie, when they married last May, even though Marie was from Coolcaslagh, just east of Killarney, and Pat had dragged her out here from London, where she'd been a nurse in the war, and *his* nurse, too – just as it was true that the ice thawed with Mother Kennedy a little with each new grandchild born. There were four so far now: two boys from Dan, a girl from Mick and another boy from Pat. The only time Brigid Kennedy approached something like contentment was when she had a baby on her hip, but it was as if she wished those babies had been born from air rather than from her children loving others. Nell hadn't been aware of the extent of all this until now, but Dan and Maureen had been waiting for approval since 1915 – since before he went off to war.

Babies didn't come easily for Nell, though. She spent the next three years in their little rented weatherboard house in Lilyfield making babies' clothes for all her new nieces and nephews. As all her brothers, one by one, took wives, she made so many jumpsuits and bloomers and smocks she could have opened her own shop.

'It'll happen when it does,' Stevie would hold her hand in the night and kiss her with ever more tenderness, but he was worried, too – for her. She needed something else to do, apart from making baby clothes in between counting out all the mysteries of life along her rosary beads and smoking cigarettes. He needed to do something to help her, other than kissing her as he left for the day and again when he returned, and taking her to the Catholic socials at Rozelle for a dance of a Saturday night. So he cooked up a bit of a plan, and one Monday evening when he came in from his office in town, he told her: 'I got you a job at the Department of Public Works – stenographer to the City Architect.'

Nell couldn't believe her ears – unless you knew someone high up, it was very difficult at that time for a woman to be employed at such a public-service job, with all the men returned from the war given preference, even in taking shorthand and typing up letters, and it was unheard of for a married woman to get so much as a look-in. When she managed

to make her mouth work, she said to her husband:
'But how?'

'Luck of the Irish.' He winked. 'All in the knowing of who to have a beer with at lunchtime.' And
then he told her: 'But you have to pretend you're
my sister.'

Her jaw dropped open again at the lie, and then
she smiled, returning her husband's wink. Oh, how
she adored him. He was only a lowly, middling clerk
in the accounts section of the Department of Lands,
but he was a king to her.

Naturally, luck of the Irish being what it is,
this all meant Nell became pregnant with their
first child within a month of starting with the City
Architect – just as she'd made two new suits for herself, too. But, luck working its strange way again,
any embarrassment at their fibbing was spared the
young couple as, the month after that, they were
compelled to leave Sydney altogether.

Stevie's father had taken ill, out on his farm
at Guyong: some sort of heart trouble. In all the
time they'd been together, Nell had never been
to the farm, and she'd only met her father-in-law
once – at the wedding – and even then, it was brief
– mercifully. For all that she knew him so little,
though, she knew well enough that he put her own

mother in the shade for vinegar on the soul – or 'shit on the liver' as Stevie would say in moments of starkest honesty. Jim O'Halligan was not a pleasant man. Nell wondered if he actually had a heart to trouble him. He had never spared the rod or become acquainted with ideas such as friendliness or for-giveness or generosity of spirit, but he was Stevie's father and Stevie was his only son.

And Stevie's only sister, Paula, had had enough of him. She arrived on their doorstep in Lilyfield one night and in floods of hot despair said, 'I can't do it anymore, Stevie. I will kill him if I spend one more day with him.' Which was fair enough, too. Paula went to Aunt Hannah over in Cooper Street to begin her life anew, at last and at twenty-seven, while Stevie and Nell made their way to Guyong to begin – well, something different.

As much as Nell was not looking forward to living under the same roof as her father-in-law, she embraced the adventure ahead – both the coming baby and the move, whatever it might bring, and for however long it might be. She hadn't known anything of the countryside since she was a small girl, back in Ballymacyarn, and after one hundred and fifty miles on the train, going up through the Blue Mountains and into the Central West hills, the scenery, at least, didn't disappoint. It was as gold and green as a Fenian flag.

Nell O'Halligan put aside that look of horror that had come over her mother's face when she'd told her they were off to the bush, and the frigid silence that had followed. She had her pebble in her shoe, Nell did, portable shame and guilt enough for a lifetime – she could go anywhere she liked! She also put aside the fact that all those years ago, when Stevie had first appeared for a term at the age of ten at school, it had been because his mother was dying from pernicious anaemia in Sydney Hospital, and he'd come alone to stay with his Aunt Hannah then, because his father wouldn't leave the farm to come, and wouldn't let his sister, Paula, come either, to say goodbye – poor Paula, just thirteen, cooking and cleaning for that miserable crank as her mother faded away. Most of all, Nell put aside the fact that Stevie, ordinarily so full of chat and cheer, sat silent on the train the whole journey, his own thoughts churning: it was only that one of the Christian Brothers had taken an interest in his potential rugby worth that Stevie had got away again at all – and now he was going back. How could he not?

'We'll make things work out well,' she told him, squeezing his hand. 'I'll see to it.'

She did her very best, but the next three years would go down as their very worst, and her loneliest. Her baby didn't come: there was a sharp pain and a rush of blood; the doctor, in Bathurst, said it simply didn't take, dismissing her from his rooms. She wondered if it was the churning that was always going on inside her that had churned the baby out. Stevie tried to offer his shoulder to her, but she wouldn't take it – he had too much on his hands dealing with his father. Jim O'Halligan would neither let go of his hold on life, than he would give over any control of the farm; he used his son as labour, tending the pigs, getting them to market, and running round for him at every harsh word. Oh but how Nell dreaded the sound of the squealing when the pigs would get carted away – they knew what was coming. Their cries reminded her of her old pet pig, back in Ireland, although she could not now remember his name.

'Dad, we've got to sell up,' Stevie would beg his father, again and again. Since Stevie had been making his way in Sydney, the farm had been badly run down as his father's health failed. The fields that for the past two decades had been planted with beet and chicory and mangold root for the pigs' winter feed was a mess – there would be no adequate crop this year. And there was no point buying in feed for the animals, only to put the farm into further debt. Even the potatoes were poor this year, the young sprouts dying back inexplicably, when ordinarily they could grow themselves in this rich earth. They had to go – they had to sell up – for all their sakes.

But Jim O'Halligan would not let go.

It was so bad Stevie even took up smoking himself.

Nell would take her little pebble out into the fields searching for solutions to problems she couldn't begin to understand. This was not her land, pretty as it might be, and she was so far from any memory of her little hands in soil, she was no practical use apart from cooking and cleaning, and milking the cow. The cow didn't even have a name – so Nell gave her one, more to spite Jim O'Halligan than anything else. She called the cow Bluebell, after the chicory flowers that were sprinkled through the paddocks. They were such lovely things, these blue flowers, blooming so sweetly out of their shabby, spindly stalks, that would rise up by midsummer shoulder-high. They became her new, giant forget-me-nots, in this new, so foreign place, and when she walked among them she would remember her own lovely father, that kind and lively colour to his eyes. She'd never known that chicory root had a blue flower. It's always funny the simple things you don't know, isn't it? When she was small, there had always been a packet of chicory powder on her mother's kitchen shelf – it's what her parents drank all through the winter, to warm them on the inside. *Healthful, economical, fragrant*, the label said around a circle, and it had a blue flower right in the middle of it. A chicory flower, of course.

Before this realisation, chicory had sat in the back of Nell's mind as a sack of rotten, twisted witches' fingers, and now it was something else again. Reborn. Replanted. So life goes; so wisdom grows.

She made daisy chains from all this chicory run to weed and she'd wind it through her hair, sprinkling sky through fire, and she'd make a crown for Bluebell, too, to make her husband laugh through all his frustrations. When she needed fabric for a new frock, she would buy the brightest floral she could find, which would elicit a grunt of disapproval from her father-in-law for such ostentatious waste, which would make her twirl as ostentatiously as she could as she went about her housework, to make her husband smile. Though it was the worst, most drifting of times, they made love like there was no tomorrow out on that farm. Away from the old, draughty, make-do homestead, she made a place for them, a warm and secret place in a corner of the hayshed, where only the chicory could hear them; and on a few precious occasions, deep in the winter, only the softly falling snow.

It was the first frosty morning of autumn 1930, when Jim O'Halligan finally let go, and let them go, too. Nell had gone out to the tankstand, as she did every morning, to fill the bucket to put water on the range for breakfast. As she waited for the bucket to fill, she was watching the ducks by the dam that sat in the front paddock – wild ducks who would come in some rhythm of seasons she still hadn't grasped. In the frost, the ducks pecked at the earth and shook their beaks as if they were having some fun time about it. She wondered if they were just enjoying the ice on their little tongues, just the same way we all do, when something made her look over her shoulder back at the homestead. She saw Stevie there, on the verandah step, and she would never know how but in just seeing him there, she knew: it was over. Their trial had finished – or this one, at least. Jim O'Halligan had died in his sleep.

She breathed out, and then she ran to her husband, leaving the tap on the tank to flow. It didn't matter, though. It was not their farm for very long to worry about after that. Stevie put it on the market, more to be rid of it than for any sensible reason, and as the Great Depression had got busy sucking the worth out of just about everything, the O'Halligan farm sold for two-fifths of a song.

So Nell and Stevie had just about nothing and no jobs to go to when they returned to Sydney that year. Only they did have one small and precious thing: Nell was pregnant again – and this time, of course, with nothing to feed it but love, their baby would come. Four of them did: Jeannie came in 1931, Carole in 1933, Beverley fast following in '34, and then Diane in '37. They all lived in a tiny flat in Petersham, between the train line and Stanmore Road, and they called it the O'Halligan Sardine Can. Stevie got work through an acquaintance he'd made at the stock-and-station agent when they were selling up in Guyong – there was a job going as a clerk in the accounts office of the Dairy Co-op in Fairfield. It was a hike on the train there and back every day, and the Sardine Can was a squeeze that got tighter every year, but these were the best years of their life together. Nell kissed her husband every morning as he left for the day, and she kissed him again on his return. They never had any money

– Nell's palms were too flat to hold any coin, she would say with a shrug – but they had got what they had wanted most.

Sometimes, Nell would get up in the night just to look at her four daughters sleeping. They made her so inexpressibly joyful, no matter what they did. For all these baby years, Nell's belly never churned – it hummed, so that she wondered if people in the street could hear it. No matter how little money they had – and with the pay cuts all the men were forced to take throughout those rough years of depression, often that money was too little to get through the month – every Saturday morning, never fail, Nell would scrimp together whatever they had to buy their roast for Sunday after mass and three pipe loaves of sweet white bread – luxury! She made two cakes a week, as well – one on Saturday, and one on Wednesday – and iced them as thickly as her budget would allow. If love could be measured out in quantities of butter and sugar, Nell would have made her family diabetic with it. She never ate more than a sliver herself, because it wasn't hers to have: it was all for them. All for the gratitude she took just in looking at them – at the icing smeared across her daughters' little hands and faces, and the crumbs in her husband's bushy blond moustache.

She wasn't making a cake or sewing bloomers, however, but out on the balcony hammering together a shelf for the girls' room, the day her mother finally visited her home. There were toys on the floor of the sitting room, and the breakfast bowls still sat drying themselves by the kitchen sink; an ashtray sat unemptied on the windowsill. Baby Diane, in her cot by the kitchen door, had just sicked up all down her bib, and Jeannie was 'helping' by taking the dirty dust cloth to her sister's face, so that Diane looked as though she had a little grey beard. It was February 1938, and it was stifling-heatwave hot; a couple of big, fat blowflies buzzed lazily through the flat, too, just to add a bit of class.

Holy Mary, Nell thought, when she opened the door and saw her mother's face. Of course she'd seen her mother often enough over the years, at every family gathering, for every wedding or christening, for the Kennedy 'colony' as her brothers now called it, but her mother had never come here – to her home. To this pigsty. Oh well, Nell shrugged, as she let her mother in. She might as well see her own daughter's love laid out as it most usually is. 'Mum,' Nell said, wondering what she might want, what criticism she might like to make first, 'this is a surprise.'

Her mother walked into the sitting room, and she walked slowly these days. She was still strong and well-made, but she was getting on. Her hair, once richly auburn, was beginning to fade to white, making her widow's black seem all the blacker. Brigid Kennedy was sixty-four years old, and for one fearful moment, Nell wondered if her mother had somehow come to say goodbye.

'What's brought you here?' Nell said, and her voice was strange, half-choked and shrill as an engine whistle.

But her mother turned with a mildly curling smile and said, 'Can't your mother visit you?'

'Of course you can,' said Nell and she said no more.

'I only want to see my grandbabies,' her mother said, picking up the little one with the grey beard, Diane, and slinging her onto her hip. 'Don't mind me – go back about your business.'

So she did, and her mother visited every second Tuesday afternoon after that – she'd take the four stops up on the train from Redfern, which wasn't too much of a trek as she'd since moved from the big house on Crown Street into a smaller one on Goodlet, nearer the station. No reason given for the change of heart; no amends directly made.

Whatever enigmatic way this thaw might have occurred, Nell wouldn't tempt it with a question. Not that Brigid Kennedy would ever forgive Stevie O'Halligan for marrying her daughter, and taking her into the bush for those three long years, but she thawed a little for him, too – enough to be quietly proud he kept his good job throughout the Depression, and was always able to pay the rent. There must have been something decent in the lad for him to have been able to see it all through.

Nell was as quietly pleased that the chain-link binding mother and daughter together, however it had come apart, was now a closed circle once more. She wanted her mother with her for the next baby, she wanted nothing more than for her mother to share that greatest adventure of life with her the whole way along. Nell wanted as many babies as God would allow, however they came. But no more would come.

Only another war did, and it would break and remake their little world, all over again.

NEWSFLASH

I've only just touched the tip of my pen to the page of my book, open on my lap, still wondering where I'm going to start my story, when the trumpets of the ABC news bulletin go off as Grandma switches on her transistor radio. It's two o'clock. I sit up straight on the edge of the sofa, about to go and join her again at the kitchen table, not because I want to listen to the boring news, but because it sounds like she might have come back from wherever she went.

When I hear what's on the news, though, I stay where I am.

'*The savage IRA sectarian murders of the ten Protestant textile workers in County Armagh a fort-night ago has caused the political leaders of Ulster to gather at the behest of Secretary of State for Northern Ireland, Mr Rees,*' the newsreader is going on. '*The killings, in themselves a retaliation for the murders of six Catholic civilians on the previous day, has prompted a meeting also of the Cabinet of the Irish Republic to discuss the worsening situation. The IRA in Armagh—'*

Grandma switches off the news, clicking her tongue and saying something under her breath that I can't quite hear; sounds like, 'stupid habit'. Any news about The Troubles that go on and on in Ireland makes her click her tongue and say something under her breath, and I know not to ask her what.

She lights another cigarette.

I go back to starting my story.

WAITING FOR HIM
TO COME HOME

'I can't sit safe out at Fairfield counting bottles of milk,' Stevie said one evening coming in from work in the summer of 1940, and it was the last thing Nell had expected.

No-one from the Kennedy clan was allowed to join up with the forces this time – Dan, who was now the patriarch with his own plumbing licence and business out at Lidcombe, would not permit it. The boys could join the coast guard or work for munitions or code-breaking telegraphy or digging ditches out at Dubbo, but they were not to leave the country to fight foes for foreigners. Absolutely no exceptions. With every year that passed, their brother Pat, who was now a solicitor with a firm in Bridge Street in town representing striking wharf workers, ailed worse and worse in his lungs from the burning of the mustard gas. Pat could hardly walk up a flight of stairs without resting halfway, and if he lost his job the government would not pay him one penny's worth of compensation for his sacrifice – not because the only reason Pat had joined up in the first place was to avoid a prison sentence for his part in running the betting shop, but because no ailing veteran ever got a penny in those circumstances. So it was decided that no Kennedy boy was going to suffer as Pat had, nor any Kennedy wife as Gwenda had over the years when Mick was struck by one of his black moods. No Kennedy boy was going to war.

Only Stevie wasn't a Kennedy. He was an O'Halligan and so by definition often difficult to fathom: as much as his father had been incomprehensibly stubborn and belligerent, Stevie was as incomprehensibly kind and dutiful. In the months leading up to the war, it had weighed heavily on him to read in the papers that the Jews of Poland and Germany were being forced out of their homes, just because of their religion; it worried him, too, to think that the Poles themselves – his fellow Roman Catholics – were now being forced to salute a Nazi dictator. But it concerned him most that all these young fellows around him – bright-eyed, bushy-tailed and bonkers – were running off headlong into disaster without enough older blokes to keep them steady. Not that Stevie was any battle-hardened veteran – all he knew about any of it was his compulsory few months of cadets almost twenty years ago now, in which he'd enjoyed running around the bush out at Ingleburn with a bunch of mates, firing off old .303s at targets rather than tin cans, the sort of thing that eighteen-year-old boys do of their own accord anyway. And the sort of thing that Stevie himself had a fairly natural talent for.

So then, it was a fatherly instinct, and perhaps not having sons of his own to shoot tin cans with, that drove him to do what he did: join up with the Australian Army, at the age of thirty-seven.

And Nell was not happy about it at all. She'd never said no to her husband before, but she said it emphatically now: 'No.'

Although he might have been mild in every other sense, Steven O'Halligan was fierce in his decency, and he replied to his wife: 'I'm sorry, Nell, but it's already done.'

There would be no further discussion on the subject. It must be remembered that this man was once the boy who had stood up to his own father at the age of ten and told him he was going to Sydney, to his Aunt Hannah, to be near his mother when she was almost at her end. He packed a bag and started walking the one hundred and fifty miles from Guyong – only one of the neighbours, Mr Graham, took him up to the train at Bathurst and gave him the fare. Now, the Dairy Co-op were giving their best accounts clerk a guarantee that he'd have his job back when he came home. Stevie was that sort of fellow: so decent that most others couldn't help being decent in return.

He spent the first two years out at Ingleburn, barely twenty-five miles from his girls, training the young fellows in how to hit targets in the bush, and since the army didn't like sending away married men with families to feed, as that would be burdensome for everyone involved, it almost looked as though he'd go no further. But then the Empire of Japan dropped their bombs on Hawaii and he soon enough got sent away. Not to rescue Poles or Jews, though. Sergeant O'Halligan got send to the jungles of New Guinea.

'Practically not even out of the country,' he reassured his wife on leaving, but Nell was far from reassured. She went into such a state of churning she could have been put to work making butter for the Co-op. For the first fortnight he was away, she smoked so many cigarettes, she'd give herself a blinding headache by lunchtime. But then she realised she had to pull up her socks and fight, too – for her sanity. So, she did the only sensible thing she could do: she went back to work for the public service – in the Department of Education, in the general typing pool. It wasn't hard to get a job this time. With all the men away, all she had to do was tell one small fib on the application form, ticking the box to say that she was unmarried, and it wasn't hard for Nell to keep at it, either. Her girls were all at school now, even tiny Diane just started, and each afternoon the little sisters would trot off like a line of paper dollies from Saint Michael's school up the end of the street to the Convent of Mercy, to help the Big Sisters make soup for the poor. It was beneficial for everyone involved.

'I don't know how you're managing to do it all, Ellen Mary,' her mother remarked to her one Saturday afternoon, as she helped her hang out the children's smalls on the balcony rack to dry. It was every second Saturday now her mother would come over to the flat in Petersham – it had to be because of Nell's job – and at her mother's comment just now and her rousing 'Ellen Mary' she was getting ready to sigh, taking it as criticism – for never having the washing done, for getting the girls too late to bed, for lying on the public-service application form and tempting the Devil in, et cetera, et cetera. Most days Nell felt she did nothing right, never her full attention on any task, always robbing Peter to pay Paul; perhaps the Devil had her right where she deserved to be. But her mother now put her old hand on her own and said: 'My daughter, you are a Kennedy through and through, putting your shoulder to it, the way you do.'

Angels fluttered a chorus of alleluias through her daughters' smalls at this high praise, and Nell had to look away for a moment to quell her emotions.

But, praise or not, it was just as well Nell had that job and some semblance of sanity to fall back on, as Stevie went missing-in-action the following June, in 1943. Up until then he'd written a note or a postcard to her almost every week for over a year, unless he warned her he'd be otherwise engaged, and in them, apart from his words of love and encouragement, he mostly detailed only the dull, repetitive nature of military life and how the only interesting things that ever seemed to occur were the multitude of tropical diseases that you could pick up. She knew he was at least half lying – and she lied right back, not telling him about the job with the Education Department, or how terrified she was sometimes in the night, so terrified she clutched her rosary beads so that they dug into the palm of her hand. But one day the letters simply stopped. In their place came a series of telegrams from the Department of Army: the first one informing her of his death; the second unapologetically amending that a few days later to missing-in-action, presumed taken prisoner; and the third informing her that as a result of an error in accounting, his pay had been suspended – which meant that the £3/6s. he'd been sending to her each month also disappeared. She wasn't in the slightest bit interested in the money – she never recalled giving it a thought. In fact, she would never be able to remember what she felt or what she did across those brief but intensely painful weeks, except that she typed a lot of letters about some changes to the New South Wales primary school curriculum, and that Carole had had quite bad gastro and had had to go to her mother in Surry Hills for a few days.

Stevie was eventually found: she received a telegram from the man himself on August the fourteenth, 1943, at three o'clock in the afternoon, saying only, *Brisbane. Resting.* It was a Saturday afternoon, but not a Mum-visit one, and she was alone when the post boy came. The girls were playing in the little yard beneath the balcony, under the mandarin tree there. Nell watched them for a while, leaning on the rail, and she knew from that moment that he was safe, that everything would be all right. She felt the warm hand of Jesus on her shoulder telling her it was so, and this was no imaginary thing: she saw the dirt beneath his fingernails.

She would never discover what had really occurred to her Stevie – that he and five of the others in his company had become separated in fighting in the Solomon Islands, caught up in the Japanese retreat. She would never know how close her husband and his comrades came to being executed as they put their hands up in surrender, the Japanese officer changing his mind and deciding his men didn't have that second to waste to get away themselves. She would never know that the toll of this and all other untold horror he witnessed in the islands and in the jungles of New Guinea meant that Stevie had to be pulled from the front, and go back to training boys in shooting tin cans, in the bush in Cowra and Coonabarabran, until his nerves came right.

When he finally came home, at Easter 1944, she knew not to ask. She knew enough: he now smoked more than she did.

He told her in careful silence on the subject, 'You don't have to worry about me, Nell. There are plenty who've had a much harder time of it.'

She knew that was the whole truth: there were always plenty who were having a much harder time of it at any one moment.

Stevie was demobbed at Easter 1946, and that was an end to it. He took no joy from the bombs that had been dropped on the ordinary people of Japan to force their surrender, but neither would he ever buy anything made in that country – not for all the days of his life would he touch something he thought a Jap might have touched before him; not a shiny new shifting spanner, not a child's tin toy, no matter how cheap they came.

He went back to the accounts at the Dairy Co-op. He watched his girls grow into young women, playing basketball for the western suburbs regional team and winning freestyle-swimming races for their school. His girls went to the best school they could afford – Bethlehem College, over in Ashfield – and they could afford to send all four of their girls right up to Leaving Certificate because Nell held onto her job at the Education Department. She was almost going to give it up – keeping up the lie of being a spinster seemed so awful with every passing year, especially when their eldest, Jeannie, got married herself in 1952, to Vic – but then her brother Pat died suddenly, from an asthma attack, they said, and Nell decided one lie was as good as another. Pat died of the injury to his lungs from German mustard gas – that's what should have been written on that particular form. Pat was the brother who had insisted upon her own education, too. She didn't know what to do with her anger at his premature and needless passing away, apart from keeping on at the typing pool, and never eating mustard on her sandwiches again.

Dear Brigid, Mother Kennedy, didn't last many months after that. Her walk slowed until she could not take the stairs of her house, never mind the train, the last strands of faint auburn in her hair turned white, but she had been independent and dignified to the end. Her funeral was attended by all of her surviving eleven sons and her daughter, and their combined brood of fifty-two children of their own – their 'full deck', as they had become known at that time. There were seven little great-grandbabies in attendance, too. So much for her to smile down on from heaven, there was not one tear shed at her farewell. She was returned to her beloved Daniel. She was two weeks and three days from turning eighty, and they buried her beside her husband at Rookwood Cemetery, under a Celtic cross.

There was too much family and too many things always going on in it for grief to bite too hard that sad day – and possibly far too much alcohol consumed at the wake as well, as Mother Kennedy had always insisted upon moderation but wasn't around now to make her displeasure known. Dan, now sixty-three years old, got so drunk his sons had to carry him home in a taxi.

As for Nell, the time soon came for her to give all fibs away in the world of men, too, as Jeannie was carrying the first of her grandchildren, and Grandma couldn't be in two places at once, could she. If her own mother, Brigid, had been partial to a bub, Nell O'Halligan made an art form out of her own devotedness. As each of her daughters married – next was Carole to Brian, and then Beverley to Geoff – Grandma Nell soon found herself in at least three different places at once. Jeannie and Vic moved out to Campbelltown, where they had a small farm, and where Vic was a vet; Carole and Brian, who was an engineer with a North Sydney firm, moved up to Turramurra; Beverley and Geoff went to Kogarah, where Geoff was an assistant planning officer with the Cumberland County Council. Oh how pleased, how constantly, beaming pleased Nell was as she darted here and there along the train lines across all of sprawling Sydney, going to her grandbabies, knowing that their fathers were all good men with good jobs, and her daughters were content in their spacious, handsome homes. She'd made all their wedding dresses; the bridesmaids', too.

She wasn't so thrilled at Diane's choice of husband, though. Diane, the youngest, took her time choosing and when she did, she married a foreigner. His name was David Boszko – and he was Polish, his parents having fled that sorely ravaged country after the war. They hardly spoke a word of English.

'Are you sure?' she asked her daughter. The last thing she wanted to do was sound like a bigot or force a rift, as her own mother had done, so she pried as carefully as she could.

'Mum.' Diane rolled her eyes at her mother's ignorance. 'We've been dating for five years – and I've known him since school.'

'Oh?' it was all news to Nell.

But it was true: David Boszko had graduated with the Physics prize from De La Salle College in 1952, and he'd been waiting and working to get himself in a position to ask Diane to marry him before he did.

'But he's only a mechanic,' Nell whispered to Stevie in the dark of night, and she could hardly believe she'd said such a snobbish thing, either. Her snobbishness was diving only lower and lower, though, the more she worried: David Boszko's mother was a cleaner at Camperdown Hospital, and his father was a concrete layer. 'How do we know Diane will be well looked after?'

Stevie, as much as he sympathised with her worry, could only laugh at this one. 'Nell. The boy's a mechanic with a university degree in automotive electricals, who's just got his own shop open on Parramatta Road. I don't think he's too backward.'

And that was true, too. David Boszko's parents had slaved to put him through university, and had even helped him get the lease on the shop – Boszko's Batteries – right among the car yards at Strathfield, in prime position. He was the only egg in their basket, and they would do anything to have him succeed.

'Besides,' Stevie turned to his wife and kissed her on the forehead, 'he's Catholic. A good Catholic kid who works hard and doesn't mind getting his own hands dirty. He'll be the one you love the most.'

That turned out truest of all. Diane's Dave would be the most considerate and thoughtful of her sons-in-law, even if he had a strange, deadpan sense of humour, and she could never tell whether he was making a joke or being serious. It must have been a Polish trait – his father, Leon, was just the same. Nell practised saying Boszko – *boshhh-ko* – and not talking to the boy's mother, Marta, as if she was deaf. She quickly fell a little bit in love with Marta's cabbage rolls, but Marta would pretend she didn't have enough English to tell her exactly what was in the sauce. Best of all, whenever Stevie looked at young Dave, it helped him to believe that, whatever the reasons his own country had sent him through hell, it had been somehow worth it to see this boy grab his opportunities here with both hands, catching the sun in his strong Polish arms.

The first of the Boszko babies came along in February 1960 – that was Shane – and Tim came in a screaming hurry after him in November '61. When Tim was born, Shane hit him over the head with a bottle of Johnsons baby powder, and things between them stayed fairly much that way from then on. Nell called them Whack and Wail. Diane and Dave only ever intended having the two, and as soon as Shane was in school and Tim in kindergarten, Diane went back to work herself, doing the accounts for Taubman's paint in York Street, in town, because they let her knock off at three. Diane was a diligent planner – neatest handwriting of anyone on earth, that girl – and she'd put all her pay away as if she'd never got it, money they would use to take the kids travelling one day, to Ireland, to Poland, and to get a proper inside bathroom put into their old and rickety Marrickville house; maybe a swimming pool for the backyard, too. Diane always had a long view.

She didn't see her surprise coming, though. Luck of the Irish and Poles combined to send her an unexpected daughter, born in September 1966. Diane, in her ever-practical, get-what-you're-given way, hadn't even picked out a name.

'Mum,' she said, 'why don't you choose?'

Nell had never felt so honoured in her life. She'd never seen such a pretty baby in her life, either, and she'd seen a lot of babies. This one had her mother's wide blue wondering Kennedy eyes but her father's dark hair, and his creamy skin that would tan in the summer. She looked like a little pixie plucked from a field of flowers on a hillside above Ballymacyarn. This one would be the last of her grandbabies, Nell O'Halligan had no doubt. There was only one name for her then, and that was Brigid Danielle – after Nell's own mother and father and the place where she was born, the place where her own heart began.

'Brigid.' Diane nodded at her tiny daughter, and at the memory of her grandmother. To Diane, Brigid Kennedy had been a statuesque figure always in black, a capable woman, strong and stern – until she smiled, passing sweets under the table to anyone who was glum. Grandmother Kennedy had a laugh that was sparingly used, but when it was it shook the world. Diane Boszko smiled at her own mother now down this centuries' long chain of love: 'Brigid, it is.'

And as that chain goes along and along, Nell often had cause to worry about all her daughters' ways over the years. She thought Jeannie spoiled her Jane, Matt and Jason too much, always saying yes to them; she thought Carole gave her Sarah and Greg too many high-and-mighty ideas; she thought Beverley let her Brad, Jen and Karen spend too much time at the beach; she thought Diane was too hard on her Shane, Tim and Bridge, such high expectations of homework and minding manners. But Nell didn't say anything to any of them in criticism. They were all doing their best, and their best was always better than any mistake they might have made. Most lovely of all, she would sometimes catch the look of wonder in Diane's eyes when she looked at her young Brigid's schoolwork, or the funny little stories she'd write on random pages in exercise books. Diane kept every scrap: folding all of it carefully into the Z pockets of her concertina family-document files, year after year.

All the while, no matter where Nell went, whatever she might have on her dance card for the day, be it a sports match or a performance at one of their schools or shopping for uniform fabric in town, she'd make Stevie his sandwiches before he left for work. She made them out of pipe-loaf bread, the best white bread, roast beef and sweet pickle. These special loaves were made by the once-famous Abbco bakery, but as the years rolled on they fell out of fashion; you couldn't get them at any general grocers, only at certain shops, and Nell went all the way to Town Hall station twice weekly to get her supply for Stevie's lunch. Circle sandwiches, one of the grandchildren once called them, she'd forgotten which one, but circles they surely were: circle after circle of unbroken devotion.

And every morning still, Stevie O'Halligan kissed his wife when he left for the day; he kissed her again in the evenings, when he returned. Stevie and Nell never made any great pile of money, they never bought a house or a car – they missed that boat, Stevie would always say, and always with a wink.

He never went past doing the accounts for the Dairy Co-op at the Fairfield warehouse; it was a safe job, and safety was all he wanted, after the things he'd seen of life's privations and cruelties. The highest up the ladder the O'Halligans ever went was to be the first in their little Petersham block of flats to get the phone put on, back in 1949, and that was all for safety, too. Humble they might have been, but their family never went without. Love. Food. Laughter. The comfort of a warm heart on a cold day: what else is there?

When Stevie was getting ready to retire, what little pile of money they had they used to build a small flat over the back of Diane and Dave's in Marrickville, in 1973. It was good for everyone, all round – especially Diane, for she could work until five pm now that she would have unhired help at home in the form of her mum. Marrickville was a bit of a shock at first, with all the Greeks and Italians having moved in there, but Nell soon discovered a liking for veal scaloppini at Papa's Italian Bistro on the corner of Illawarra Road, and made friends with the Greek *yia yia*, Vicki Angelopoulos, next door.

Stevie was seventy-two years old and still not quite retired at Christmas, 1975. He'd received a beautiful silver watch from the Co-op in anticipation of it, though. The new bookkeeper they had employed – a fellow called Terry Barnsley who was studying accountancy at night at university, and who Stevie had interviewed himself and recommended to the board as a bright young bloke – couldn't cope if ever it got busy. The place would be in a mess in five minutes, with suppliers unpaid, and deliveries delayed. Stevie was beginning to think he'd backed the wrong horse – his heart had always been soft, but maybe his mind was getting soft, too. This young fellow had seemed keen to get ahead, but maybe he was too keen to do that without too much actual working.

As it was, it meant Stevie was back at the job straight after Christmas, on December thirtieth, to rescue Terry from himself when the orders rushed in between the public holidays. For the first time ever, as he got ready that morning, he wondered if he could be bothered. The earth wouldn't stop turning if he didn't go in. The lad would just have to learn to stand up to the job.

He sighed as Nell handed him his lunch bag, packed with his sandwich and a peach, today. He kissed her as he always did, and winked as he'd wink a hundred times: 'I'm not going to do this again.'

Nell laughed – at him. She said at the door:

'Take your raincoat – it's going to rain.'

He shook his head. 'I won't shrink if it does. See you about seven, I'd say.'

It started raining at about eleven that morning and it rained on and on nonstop all day. Unlike the usual summer rain, which came in crashing, evening bursts, this was more like a midwinter drizzle. It was oddly chilly, too. Nell had felt her spirits dampen with the weather, and although she'd meant to pay a visit to her brother Dom, who was nearing eighty, half-deaf and fading fast, she couldn't imagine getting on the train and going all the way to his house in Epping. She'd felt stuck to her chair in the kitchen, and all day her head ran through with morbid thoughts. Five of her brothers were gone now – in order of disappearance, Pat, Mick, Dan, Chris and Frank; two of her friends from mass had died in the last month, too. She lit yet another cigarette, as if it might push death away.

It was nearing six o'clock, and she felt her stomach churning over and over, round and round – *nothing*, she told herself. *I'm a silly old woman. Steve'll be home in an hour or so.* In between the decades of her rosary meditations, round and round prayers for each of her babies, she concentrated on letting the sound of her husband's laughter run through her mind. She smiled at a memory of Christmas just gone: over a beer, he and Leon had been discussing the fors and againsts of communism, and when Stevie had wondered if Gough Whitlam's trouble had been that he went too far or didn't go far enough in making laws fairer for ordinary people, Leon had replied that Gough Whitlam wouldn't know communism if it confiscated his silver spoon. Stevie, who always seemed tuned in to Leon's jokes, laughed so hard at that one, the sound seemed suddenly now to fill the room.

Only to fall as suddenly quiet once more. She listened to the rain hitting the window. She listened to her grandsons Shane and Tim knock something over downstairs – possibly one of the dining chairs. Little Brigid shrieked out: 'Stop it!'

Diane must have been busy somewhere else in the house, so Nell got up to investigate. Halfway down the stairs, she heard a knock at the door.

Then she heard Diane open it.

As Nell stepped into the hall at the foot of the stairs, she saw the policeman standing there, asking her daughter: 'Is Mrs Ellen O'Halligan here?'

IRISH COFFEE

I wake up with the afternoon sun making a hot line of light across my face, and I'm confused for a minute. I've fallen asleep on the sofa, and I didn't realise I had. My pen has stuck to the side of my face. I didn't get very far with my story, I know that. My book has fallen down the side of the sofa, between the cushions, and I pick it up to see I've only drawn a peacock feather on it, while I was thinking about what to write. I've done the floaty, stringy bits of the feather in green ink, and a little circle of red at the top, waiting to be coloured in blue. My pen is a clicker pen with the four colours – red, green, black and blue – and the blue has run out. I'd like another one, but they're expensive. Grandma would get me one, if she knew I needed it, but I don't want to ask her for a silly thing like that, not today. She won't want to go to the newsagents now anyway. I'll ask to borrow her blue pen, later.

She's still sitting in her chair, on her side of the table in the kitchen. I don't have to look up and turn around to check she's there. I can see her cigarette smoke swirling through the air: it always swirls along in the same direction, from the kitchen across the sofa and towards the radiogram, which sits by the door that leads out to the back steps that go down into the yard. Granddad's door. He'd always leave and come home by that door, never the front door downstairs. I'm only nine, but I know Grandma is waiting for him now. It makes me want to cry, but I know I should never do that.

Maybe we should watch some TV. Yes – that's a good idea. I should ask Grandma if she wants to watch *Columbo*, the detective show – there've been repeats on at half past three every afternoon all week, I've checked the guide in the paper. It's one of my favourite things to do with Grandma, just us, watching her grown-up TV shows, while Mum's still at work in town. 'Don't tell your mother I let you,' Grandma says as she pulls me to her whenever she lets me have a sneaky look in the holidays. Mum doesn't let me watch commercial TV – not because of the shows, but because of the ads. She doesn't want them getting into my head to rot my brain. I don't watch the commercials, or the shows that much, anyway. I never get the clues and guess the murderer in *Columbo* – the stories are always much more complicated than my *Nancy Drew* mysteries, and you don't get a chance to read back over things to see where you are – but I listen to the sounds Grandma's stomach makes as we snuggle on the sofa together. It's always talking, her stomach: it's never still or quiet. I'm still not sure if I should interrupt her now, though. She puffs out her cigarette smoke with a swoosh that sounds like she's angry, but it's only her concentrating sound. The sound she makes if she's puzzling over a new sewing pattern, or the cryptic crossword.

But now I look behind me, over the armrest of the sofa, and under the edge of the tablecloth I see the crucifix of Grandma's rosary swinging against her pink skirt, as she pinches and pushes the beads through her hand with her thumb.

There's something not right about this. I don't know what it is. She's going too fast through her prayers, she is pinching the beads too hard, like she really is angry. I sit up now. I don't blame her that she's angry, she must be angry, but you can't be angry when you are saying your rosary. It's not right. You're supposed to be contemplating the Blessed Mysteries – the Joyful Mystery, the Sorrowful Mystery, the Glorious Mystery, and the Luminous Mystery. I don't even know what those mysteries are yet, but I know if you're angry, you spoil the whole thing – that's what Grandma has told me herself, as well as Sister Gabriel at school, who knows everything. *Hail, Holy Queen, Mother of Mercy, our life, our sweetness and our hope! To thee do we cry, poor banished children of Eve.* It's supposed to bring you peace and soothe your worried mind. But Grandma is so angry, she doesn't even notice me stand up right in front of her now.

I notice she's washed up our lunch things and made her coffee – she always makes a cup of Instant Café at four o'clock – but she's left it on the side of the sink to go cold. This is wrong. She's still staring and staring out the window, towards town. Just staring, staring, staring, over the yard and out at the city. I have to find a question to ask her, something to make her look at me. Her lips are pressed together too tight as she keeps pushing and pinching at the beads in her lap. She's frightening me. I have so many questions going around and around in me. Where has Granddad gone? Does heaven really exist? What is a stroke? Did Granddad slip and hit his head in the rain? Is that what hurt him? But I can't ask any of these questions that might only make her sadder. Angrier.

Instead, I look at the coffee again. Maybe I should make her a fresh one. Or a whiskey. She always has her coffee at four o'clock, but she always has a whiskey at six – she lets me suck the peppery ice cubes when she's finished. Grandma loves her evening whiskey; just the one. Her little silver nip measure sits by the biscuit tin on the kitchen bench; the whiskey is at the top of the tall cupboard next to it. Maybe she'd like an Irish coffee; Mum sometimes has one of them after dinner – that's black coffee with whiskey in it, topped with a dollop of cream. But I don't know how to make it, not really – Mum's coffee is proper coffee, whatever that is, made in a pot on the stove, somehow. I don't even know how to make an everyday Instant Café from the tin. And that makes me want to cry again. I can't do that.

'Grandma.' Her name smashes from me like I've dropped a plate, and I ask her: 'Can you show me how to make a coffee?'

For one horrible second I think she can't hear me, that she's really gone somewhere very far away, but then slowly she turns her head and she sees me.

Her big blue eyes look at me like she didn't catch what I said, but then she asks me: 'Coffee? Why do you want to make a coffee? That's not for little girls.'

I point to the cup on the sink: 'Your coffee. I thought it might be cold sitting there. Do you want me to make another one for you?'

'Oh?' She looks at the cup there, too. She says: 'I'd forgotten I'd made that at all. I'm getting old.'

'Can I help make another one?' I ask her, and I beg her with my own eyes: *you're not old. You're beautiful – more beautiful than anyone else's grandma. When I grow up I'm going to dye my hair the same colour as yours.* Grandma turned seventy on New Year's Day; we didn't have cake or presents, but I love the shape of that number – I hid my drawing of it inside my Scooby-Doo colouring book.

And she looks at me with a little frown, but with a small smile, too: 'I suppose you can help me make a cup of coffee. You're big enough that you should know how to pour hot water safely.'

She puts her rosary back in the pocket of her skirt, and she puts the kettle back on, too, and as she moves around the kitchen, I keep trying to find more questions to ask, to keep that little smile coming back onto her face.

'What's coffee?' I ask her next, picking up the

tin of Instant Café. 'The smell of it is so nice.' And it really is.

There's a small smile in her voice now as she says: 'I'm not sure how much of that is coffee. Coffee beans are very dear, but this stuff isn't – you wouldn't know what was in it.'

'What would be in it if it's *not* coffee?' I keep up my asking.

'Sawdust and nail filings,' Grandma says, rinsing out the cup.

'No. That's not true.' I know she's pulling my leg. 'What do they really put in it?'

She looks across her shoulder at me and there's even a little bit of a smile in her eyes as she says: 'Chicory. During the war it was just about all chicory that went into coffee tins, but it's probably got more coffee in it now than it did then.'

I know not to ask about the war – I've been told that a hundred times, from Mum *and* Dad. If any of my grandparents mention it, you just shut up and listen and don't ask any stupid questions. Granddad did something in the jungles in New Guinea, shooting at Japanese; Papa Leon went to prison for trying to blow up Germans in Warsaw, in Poland, but he got caught – that's what Shane told me. So I ask Grandma next: 'What's chicory?'

'Chicory? It's a plant, with a tall, pretty blue flower and a great long root like a witch's finger.' She wriggles her finger at me and I can feel my smile like sunshine all over my face. She smiles back, a proper smile with all her wrinkles showing, and she tells me now: 'They dry the roots and grind them up into a fine powder – the people who make chicory powder, that is, not the witches.'

I laugh and she tells me more: 'Once upon a time, your great-grandmother Brigid loved the stuff. Just plain chicory, mind you – no coffee at all. There was no such thing as pure coffee in Ireland back in those days. Only specks of coffee sprinkled into chicory – but mostly only plain old chicory. It came in a paper package, and it was always sitting above the stove in our cottage, on the farm, in Ballymacyarn – and it was a luxury in itself, imported from America. Mother Kennedy drank it every winter when I was a little girl. But it's out of fashion now. Now, chicory is just a weed.'

'What's a weed?' I ask her, and I'm only asking because I know it's the stupidest question.

'You're a little weed.' My grandmother plays along with me, and I'm so happy, I want to squeeze her to me round her pink skirt, to keep her with me.

But I ask her instead, to keep her playing: 'Why am I a weed?'

And she tells me: 'You have blue eyes like forget-me-nots, Brigid Boszko, blue eyes like chicory. You're at least half weed. Irish – common and wandering.'

I don't know what she means, but she looks away, back out the window, and she starts staring again. The kettle clicks off as it finishes boiling, but she keeps staring. And now I can't help it: my tears bubble up into my eyes and crack out of my throat.

That makes Grandma stare at me: 'Why are you crying, Brigid?'

She looks like she can't believe what she's seeing. I don't know if I'm in trouble or not, if I've done the wrong thing, but I suppose I have, so I tell a fib to try to stop the mess I'm making.

I shrug. 'Oh, you know, just when you say my whole name like that – Brigid Bozsko. The other kids at school tease me about it – they call me Bozo.' I don't even care that they do, no-one says it in a mean way, but it sounds like a dumb thing to be crying about, and in the middle of the holidays when I'm not seeing anyone from school much except Sharon over the road, who never says anything interesting. At least my name is not Voula Boosalis – she gets called Hula Hoops, and it makes her really upset, but that doesn't make them stop teasing her in the playground. Thinking about Voula stops my tears, though. Nearly.

Grandma is not fooled; she says: 'That's not why you're crying – tell me the truth. What are you upset about?'

So now it rushes out: 'I'm sad that you're so sad, Grandma. I'm frightened when you stare out the window.'

Grandma frowns sharper at that, and her voice is sharp at me, too: 'What are you frightened of?'

'I don't know.' I keep crying – it won't stop now. I'm sure I'm in trouble but I can't lie to my grand-mother, either. I tell her: 'I'm frightened that you're too sad.'

'Too sad?' Grandma says and I think she doesn't believe me even now I have told her the truth. She blinks at me. Our blue, tired eyes blink at each other. Our eyes are the same: everyone says so. I think she's going to tell me to shoo, to stop addling her again. But now she grabs me to her pink skirt. 'Oh my baby girl,' she says as she holds my head against her stomach. 'My sweet Bridgey girl. I'm sorry I frightened you.' She pulls me with her onto her kitchen chair by the window. 'Come here. Don't cry. Grief – it's such a terrible, sinful thing. Let me tell you a story, then – let me tell you one I've never told you before. Let me tell you a story about some weeds. Two hundred years of grief, and weeds.'

A TROUBLESOME
CROP

The wind rushed cold and lonely over the hills that rolled out from Slieve Gullion, the high rebel country between Mullaghbawn and Drumintee, in the south of County Armagh. It was the year 1690, all of Ulster had been long stolen by the English, its people forced into servitude, and Seamus O'Halligan, as he stood amid the heather atop that slieve, was debating in himself what he should do.

The O'Halligans had called these hills home since King Fergus had lost them to the Chieftains of Airgíalla, more than a thousand years ago, but whatever thief it was that staked his stained and ragged flag into this earth, Seamus would never surrender. He was only a lowly farmer, a keeper of pigs, but this was his land, and he would defend it – this slim scrap of it that was left to him. It was land his own father had given up his life for: six summers ago, when Seamus had been not much more than a boy, there had been an accusation made that the O'Halligan pigs had got into the neighbouring cornfields down in the valley – fields owned by English planters – and his father was condemned to hang for it by a judge and jury made up, of course, only of English planters. No chance to defend himself; no means to prove that it had been planters' pigs that had done the damage to the corn. That was justice under the English Crown.

These English thieves were Protestants, and they considered the Irish to be little more than savages, as they considered all Catholics to be, and they made many laws against them – as they made laws against Catholics in every land they sought to conquer. And so it was that a great war exploded now across not only Ireland, but all of Europe.

Seamus O'Halligan did not care for all this sectarian squabbling; he cared even less for the game of power at play, with the Protestants wanting the Dutchman, William of Orange, to be King of the British Isles instead of King James, who was William's father-in-law as well as his nephew, and cousin of the King of France. It was impossible to reason out the purpose of it all, much less follow who was related to whom, or who was presently on the throne. Seamus was not much more inspired by his own religion, either. He was Catholic, no doubt about it, but he was a child of these hills before he was a child of any God: the souls of all his grandfathers harked back to a time before Saint Patrick had brought any Cross to this country at all. For Seamus, these very hills were his religion: the mountainside he stood upon, the whole of Slieve Gullion, was a spine atop a dragon's tale, and the lake that sat between the ancient cairns on its peak, was home to a witch whose wisdom he sought out now.

The Cailleach Bhéarach, she was called in his language. She was daughter of Oisin, the warrior poet; she was queen of this mountain and every fae spirit that lived upon it. Her name was Miluchrach, and she would answer his questions.

Should he leave his land to fight the Williamites for King James? Should he take up arms with James' army – the Jacobites? Would he see Ireland freed from tyranny if he did? Would he see this land returned to the O'Halligans, by legal right, once more?

The water of the lake was still. The chill wind that had just now been wild through the trees and through his hair was suddenly quiet as well. Clouds behind him parted and the sun was warm upon his shoulders. The white flowers of early summer spread out from the lake like a scattering of snow, bushes of field roses and dewberries sprawling over the ground. A great heron then flew through the sky above him, broad silver wings reflected in the surface of the water. The bird cried out across the hills. Seamus looked up, to watch where it went, and it kept on, south-east, until it disappeared from his sight. South-east: the direction of Dublin, the heart of Erin, the direction that William of Orange was going. Miluchrach of the lake had spoken: it was time for Seamus O'Halligan to get going, too.

'No!' said his wife, Nuala, when he returned to his house and his family. 'Don't go – it's madness. King William has already won.'

Seamus looked around at his house: it was not much more than a hovel of hastily gathered stone and thatch and rotting daub. Once, the O'Halligans, and all their *mhuintir – their* people – had lived in fine cottages, dotted along the hillsides and all through the valleys this side of the mountain as so many dewberry blooms. His grandfather's stables had been a finer building than the one Seamus was forced to keep his own family in now. He knew his wife was right; the evidence was all around him. The English had won this argument a long time ago, whatever priest they sent to pass judgement over Ulster's remains. Year after year, more and more of his own fellows – Irishmen – were renouncing their faith and their so-called savagery, converting to Protestantism, to get along. But Seamus did not give that course one moment's consideration. He would not – he *could* not – admit defeat.

'Please,' Nuala begged him. 'Be grateful for what we have. Look into the eyes of your son and tell him you won't leave him.'

Seamus O'Halligan looked into the eyes of his little boy, not two years old, and it gave him only more reason to go. This boy was all of why he had to fight – why he would die, if that was to be his fate.

And so he made his goodbyes. He loved his Nuala as only true lovers can, and with his body he made his farewell to her at the edge of the forest, in the warmth of the afternoon; she threaded a field rose into the breast of his coat and she told him: 'You will come back.'

She went up to the mountaintop alone then; she begged the fae ones and their witch: let him come back or it is me who will die. She cut her long golden hair off with a knife and scattered it across the waters of the lake. For she loved her husband more than land, or air, or bread, or pride.

He took their only horse and began his journey south towards Dublin, a distance of sixty miles from Slieve Gullion, and on the way, as he passed through the village of Drumintee, he was told that the forces of William of Orange were now at Drogheda, at the River Boyne; that the Jacobites lay in wait on the far bank, too. A battle would be waged there, and soon.

Drogheda was only half the distance to Dublin – only thirty miles – and Seamus urged his horse on through night and day to get there, out through the rolling drumlins and lakelands of his own county and down along coast that looked across the Irish Sea, towards the land of his enemy. Not that he could see much of them when he arrived at the river. A mist had rolled in from that sea, and sat heavily in the glen that enfolded the bank to the north. He could hear them, though: a vast troop of many languages – English, of course, and there were Dutch and Danish, French Huguenots and Scots Gaels, too. But Seamus was not afraid: wasn't the mist clothing him as he rode right by this army of Orangemen?

He crossed the river at the town and if anyone noticed him, he looked like any other traveller.

There was no uniform to mark him out as a soldier. There was no uniform for any Irish Jacobite. They were poor men, all just as he, in desperate need of some victory, however slight. When Seamus found his fellows to the south of Drogheda, he knew them by this poverty: they carried scythes, not swords; slingshots, not guns. They were fifteen thousand strong and more, but they were an army of sticks and stones. As he stood among the swelling numbers of men, he knew his wife was right again: this was madness.

As a horseman, Seamus was furnished with a matchlock musket, and his company would lead the charge up to the Orangemen across the shallow ford. If he was terrified by now, the drums overtook the pounding of his heart and charge he did. The enemy he saw that day might have been Englishmen; they might have been Dutch, or Scots. He'd never know. He saw their faces through the mist of gun smoke, and they all looked like mad men: they all looked like him. He found his wisdom far too late, for as he fumbled at his musket, the faster, surer shot of a Danish flintlock pistol sent its bullet straight through his chest.

He fell from his horse and the battle went on around him. As he died, there in the shallows of the Boyne, he smelled the sea on the breeze coming in again from the south-east and thought he saw a woman walk towards him through the rushing and wheeling of hooves – beautiful, she was, tall, her golden hair unwound about her. He wished it was Nuala, but he knew it was Miluchrach, the witch. She knelt down to him and took the rose from his coat, the rose his wife had set there, white petals now stained red with his blood, and she put it to his lips as he took his final breath.

King James took himself all the way back to France in hasty retreat, and King William went on to Dublin as the bodies of a thousand Irishmen and more lay dead and unremembered in the softly falling rain. Outnumbered and ill-equipped as they were, they'd never stood a chance.

Their souls might well have gone direct to the saints in reward for all their courage, but even if they did, it meant nothing to Nuala. Every time her little boy asked her where his father had gone, every time she felt the new baby kick inside her womb, the knives of grief came for her.

Widowed, penniless and powerless, in the year that followed, she was forced from their little home in the hills, and into the township of Armagh to seek alms. What she did there to feed her two sons across their growing years is no-one's business but Miluchrach's; no matter what she did, though, those years saw Nuala's boys stripped of every last right they might have had in their own country – this land of all their grandfathers. Catholics across all Erin now were prevented by law from receiving any education, prevented from the purchase of any land or from holding any public office. They had no right to own a horse worth more than five pounds, and if you were fortunate enough to own some scrap of dirt somewhere, you had to split it between all your sons until there was none left, down and down the line until it disappeared. If they spoke their language in the street, they would be spat upon and beaten.

Nuala O'Halligan never married again. She never smiled again, either. Instead, her tears laid down a curse, a wail of mourning that would haunt the O'Halligans for the next two hundred years.

*

And so it was that grief passed down and down the O'Halligan line, through all its sons, all wild and angry men of Armagh. Yes, if legend says County Kerry was the birthplace of Erin's song, it might perhaps be said that Armagh was the birthplace of her violence. But while it's true that violence never comes to anything except more violence, like a river it always has its source, seeping up through the rocks of hardship and despair.

From the great grain famine of 1740 that killed two million, to the bloody rebellion of 1798 that saw men burnt alive, their women raped and slaughtered, hatred was pounded into the souls of all O'Halligan men, generation by generation. Bile spewed from every pulpit in the land as Jesus wept and wept for each and all of His children.

By the middle of the 1800s the country was a disaster from head to toe, from arse to elbow, from Donegal to Cork, but the Devil had more coming: he had another famine to inflict. This time it would blight every potato in every field over six long years, and this time, when the English did not lift a finger to help those who lay so helpless and starving in their realm, anyone could have been forgiven for thinking that the Irish might at this point have been exhausted well past hatred. But that was not the case. A scorching hatred like no other filled every empty belly.

And so it was into these circumstances that another young Seamus O'Halligan was born. His father, Malachi, hungry and angry both, had taken violence as his profession, and with some enthusiasm. A strongman for the Republicans, he enjoyed nothing more than becoming roaring drunk and ripping into greedy landlords whenever they dared to turf unfortunates out into the streets. Malachi O'Halligan was mightily made, a monstrous giant of a man, with a mentality to match. There was no gentleness about this man: he relished his size and he used it to crush and to smash. There was no doubt he killed a few men in his day – he certainly stole from them.

He terrified his young son, Seamus, for his thrashings and his unreadable temper. In fact, the whole of Armagh terrified young Seamus O'Halligan – it seemed no week could pass without a bashing of some poor tenant farmer, or a hail of rocks hurled across the marketplace, a riot always threatening to ignite. Like his father, he was built to pull oxcarts, but unlike his father he was quiet, thoughtful. Brooding. Despite the horrors that raged on around him, though, he was not plagued too much by nightmares; instead he dreamt of pigs and fields of grain. He never knew where those dreams came from: vivid, clear; he could smell the corn reaching up towards the sun. Perhaps one of his grandmothers or aunties had told him, when he was very small, that the O'Halligan pigs had once laid claim to all the hills between Mullaghbawn and Drumintee beneath the sheltering arms of the slieve. Something was calling to the lad. Perhaps it was that great-great-great-great grandfather Seamus from so very long ago, his restless soul searching out from the ancient, enchanted mountaintop, his wounded heart in need of a home — somewhere. Somewhere far away from this broken land.

Whatever it was, the call was soon enough irresistible. One morning, much like any other, he was walking out from the centre of the township of Armagh on errand for his father — on this occasion to deliver a small package of cash to one of the deacons of the church for the never-ending construction of Saint Patrick's Roman Catholic Cathedral that lay to the west — when he heard a woman sobbing as he went by down the road. She was just out of sight beyond the darkened doorway of a cottage, a humble place of stone and rotting daub. He might have known her, or he might not have, he didn't care, and yet he would never be able to say what compelled him to do as he did next, except for the wretched sound of those tears.

He looked ahead down the road, to the spires of Saint Patrick's, the Catholic; behind him lay the medieval stone of the former Saint Patrick's, that of course now belonged to the Protestant Church of Ireland. Two cathedrals with the same name, and the same God, tearing the town, tearing the country apart, and at the realisation of this absurdity, he could stand the sound of that woman's sobbing no more. He threw that package of cash into the doorway of her cottage, and he walked on. Without a word to his own mother, and certainly without a word to his father, he kept walking – all the way to Dublin, a distance of almost ninety miles.

Along the way, he changed his name to Jim, the English shortening of James, of which Seamus was the Irish equivalent anyway. It was the year 1880, and Jim O'Halligan – thoughtful, brooding, wondering, wandering boy – was only seventeen.

At the Port of Dublin, he looked across the Irish Sea. He could not see at all where he was going, except away from all the strife and sorrow here.

*

When he heard the name Australia, he knew it only as a place of punishment, for his own great-grandfather had been sent there for running guns during the Irish Rebellion – a badge his father Malachi had worn with pride beside his own green ribbon – so

Jim O'Halligan did not especially wish to go there himself. Go there he would, though. Within a fortnight of pestering every captain and every bosun he could find along all of Dublin's quays, young Jim by his seriousness and his size won passage as a general do-all on a schooner bound for Liverpool, carrying a cargo of whiskey and lace. On board this ship – and it was called the *Rising Star* – he discovered by pure chance in overhearing a conversation among the ratings, that land in New South Wales could be got for as little as £1/5s. per acre. He also discovered the ship was sailing on for Sydney once out of Liverpool.

'Where exactly is Sydney in the world?' young Jim asked them, and he ignored their laughter at his not knowing, only waiting to hear the answer, in his gravely determined way.

'In New South Wales, you idiot,' he was told, and they dragged him over to the map that sat under glass on the forecastle wall. 'About as far south-east from Dublin as a man might go.'

As far away in any direction sounded like it might suit Jim. He traced a finger along the route south-east and when he saw it really ended at New Zealand, he asked the men: 'What's the price of an acre here?'

'Don't know.' They shrugged, but one said: 'Best grazing country on the globe – best country for butter and wool out there.'

And for all that Jim knew practically nothing about farming, that was his mind made up. He said: 'I'm not after the best. I want country good enough for raising pigs.'

At which the men only laughed at him again, another telling him: 'No wonder you don't drink – you don't need to, you weird bastard.'

He shut his mouth altogether from then on, keeping his dreams to himself. He told them only to the creaking of the timbers and the rigging, sent them up into the sparkling night skies upon that long, long sea, sent them out to whomever might heed them. Jim O'Halligan dreamed of his fields, sure that the more he dreamed them the sooner they would be found.

It took a long time – seven years carting fresh produce between the railhead and Paddy's Market in Sydney – before he saved the money to purchase his land. If times were ever rough, and they often were, he never looked back to the old country. Occasionally, in darkest times, he did think of his poor mother in Armagh, but he did not think on her for long. He could not. She had three other sons, all of them as battered and bullied as any ever were by his father, and Jim himself would not be one. He clothed himself in that grey cloak of relief at being gone from him, and that was all. Yes, he was a hard man himself, Jim O'Halligan, and mean with every penny, too. He had to be.

Deliberate and careful in his every act, and with his ear to the ground at the markets for a bargain, he bought his first parcel of acres in the rugged but fertile high country that lay between the towns of Bathurst and Orange, out west from the city. It was at a place called Guyong – a place he'd never heard of before, and had baulked at initially for the name of nearby Orange. Was it a Protestant town? It was, just as Bathurst was Catholic, but the only trouble that went on out there, he was assured, was on the football field between their rival teams. It was rich potato country, he was also told, and most importantly what was good for potatoes, he learned, was also good for pigs. He spent seven more years saving and learning before he was ready to make his long-held dream come true: to purchase his pigs, to build his home among the hills. But then, just as he was ready to go, fortune smiled on him like it had never done before: the market for both land and pigs crashed in the trade depression of 1894, and he was able to get more than he had ever hoped of each so cheap he might have thrown his hat into the air with glee.

But he did not. He had no time or cause to be content, or so he reckoned. There was too much more to accomplish now, too many decisions to make. Where best would he build his dam? What feed would he sow for his pigs? As always for Jim, much thought went into these things. The grain of his dreams, he'd realised, would not be an ideal crop for his animals, as it was expensive to grow and unreliable to harvest; his pigs and he would thrive instead on a diet of root vegetables, and so all the fors and againsts of every root had to be considered before Jim could decide which he would plant, and when he'd decided that mangold, chicory and beets would be his crop, he had to decide then how much of each he would plant and where in his acres he would plant them, then who he would trust to sell him good seed. He was often more weary at the end of each day from all these concerns than he was from all the labour of farming.

Jim had been warned by a few other farmers against putting any chicory in for his pig feed. 'It'll only run to weed all through your paddocks,' he was told. 'Troublesome stuff. Near impossible to dig out once it's in,' they said. But when they told him it was lacking in nutrition and couldn't be sold on if ever there was an over-abundance, Jim knew they were lying to him. Chicory, it was true, was certainly not for the slovenly farmer – it needed to be diligently managed. But chicory, of all the feed he put in to his fields, would bring him a small profit in itself in a good year. Jim had done his research; the other farmers just didn't want the competition. So, he planted twice as much chicory as anything else, and reaped the rewards, year after year. He sold his excess at five pence per pound – better than anyone else in the district – and once, when he had a really big bumper crop, he slaved day and night cleaning it off for best price and made eight shillings per hundredweight. That year he made almost £56 in pure profit. His pigs did very well on it, too.

And yet none of this gave him any pause to feel the slightest sweet breeze of contentment. He had all that he wanted, but he could not see where he was. Almost every afternoon, the sun would blaze down through the wide arms of the eucalypt trees on his western boundary, turning their leaves to black lace against a sky gone wild with great splashes of every colour of the rainbow. But he never saw it. Occasionally he marvelled that the rainfall in this high country was higher than he'd ever known in Ireland, but puzzlingly there was twice as much sunshine too. It was a farmer's paradise, but still Jim O'Halligan could not know it as such.

In 1900 he married, more because he thought he ought to than for any need to share his bounty. He advertised his eligibility through St Canice's at the nearby village of Millthorpe, where he attended mass only often enough as would be seen to be decent, and it wasn't long before a suitable match was arranged. He was thirty-seven years old, and the girl, Mary Ann McCall, was just gone twenty-two. She was soft-spoken and obedient, and although he cared for her in every practical sense, he never knew her. He never knew that she could laugh or dance; he never knew how the sun kissed her flaxen hair of an afternoon as she bent to tend the garden or milk the cow. He never knew how she wept with the great splashing wildness of her joy when her children came: first a girl, Paula, and then a little boy, Steven. They were the roses on each of her cheeks, those children were; they were the brightness of her smile.

There was one fleeting moment, when the boy was born, that Jim thought it strange he felt no lightness of spirit as men are supposed to do at the birth of a son. But he dismissed it as quickly: there was work to be done. Always so much work on the farm, so that he did not notice when his wife began to ail. He did not see her skin grow pale, or her smile begin to dim. He would only become annoyed at her increasing weakness.

For the darkness of the cloud Jim O'Halligan carried about him lay right across his eyes; a cloud that never stormed to release its rain. A ghostly cloud of grief that he could never articulate, much less see the trail it left, two hundred years in length.

He could not see that the little boy, Steven, planted in this grow-anything soil – as far to the south-east as an O'Halligan had ever gone – had taken on the sun and shed that trail of grief. Jim would watch him with some curiosity and even envy, but he could never fathom his child's cheerful disposition. He often took the boy's own bright smile for insolence and beat him for it. Jim could not see that he beat his son just as his own father had done, down and down the line.

But no matter how often or how brutally young Stevie was beaten, his smile could not be robbed from him. He would only try harder at whatever there was to try: football, mathematics, football, cricket and football. For he had promised his mother, as she lay dying, that he would never grieve while he could instead be grateful for being alive. It was a promise he held fast to, whatever his life would bring.

The man called Stevie O'Halligan would always be that little snowy-haired boy with the sun in his eyes, running and laughing through a chicory field, midsummer seeding and four-feet high. Why did the spell break here, with him? Why did the fae ones let him be? No-one will ever know the reason but that Stevie himself chose to break free.

AWAY ON THE
SWEET BREEZE

'Clean your teeth!' Mum shouts at me as I bolt across the hall and up the stairs, on my way to shout my 'good morning' at Grandma.

I don't stop at anything Mum says. I reckon I'm pretty good stuff, and I'm too happy. It's the last week of school – no more primary school forever after Thursday. I'm twelve and now that I'm here, I can't wait to get to high school next year. Not for the boys, though. I still hate boys, except for David Bowie, and maybe Daryl Braithwaite. I want to get to high school because you get to study poetry there, and mad history – like the Emperors of Rome and the Chinese Opium Wars. I've just finished reading Dad's copy of Frank Hardy's *Power Without Glory* and although I didn't understand half of it, I've got so political I stayed up last night and wrote a letter to the Prime Minister, Malcolm Fraser, telling him people are more important than money. Mum said I should be careful making my opinions too loudly known, but I know Grandma will laugh her little giggle laugh and tell me I'm brave and clever.

I swing round from the top of her stairs to the door of her room, and I always get a funny feeling when I do. I know I'm too old to sleep with her anymore – I've been too old since I was ten – but somehow it always seems wrong that I don't.

Something seems wrong before I even see her today. Something is too quiet here. Grandma is usually up already, and doing the crossword, waiting for me. She says that when you get to a certain age you can stay in bed and read and do the crosswords as long as you like.

I think she's still asleep. Her eyes are closed, her hands are folded over her stomach – that's just how she looks when she's asleep. Her hair isn't red anymore; she let it go white after Granddad died. Her white curls circle her face, her head hardly makes a dent in the pillow – yes, that's exactly how she looks when she's asleep. Her pretty little bird head on her pale-green pillowslip; Jesus looking down on her from his crucifix.

It's warm up here in the flat. It's going to be another hot December day, so I go back out and open the window above the sofa, to let the breeze in. I look round the flat: everything else seems normal: the kitchen is tidy; cup rinsed on sink; ashtray empty and cleaned. I look out the window at the dirty city sky: it looks like someone tipped an ashtray on it. A train screeches into Marrickville station; the brakes of a bus squeal down on Illawarra Road.

I should wake her up. I am running late now.

'Grandma?'

She's not asleep. I know she's not asleep.

She's gone. Away.

I don't know what happens for the rest of this day. I don't think I am crying. It's worse than that. It's like all the stories, our stories, are falling out of my head.

AND THEN DOWN
THE LANE

I stop the car on the track when it happens again, for the third time – this odd shiver running through me, as if I have been here before. But I couldn't have been. The map on my phone remains as it was when I last looked at it two minutes ago: Graham's Lane, wherever that might be, somewhere between Millthorpe and East Guyong. Why does this all look so familiar to me? A dirt track snaking through hills, an old, decaying hayshed, a line of brown cows along a fence looking at me with a query: and who, may we ask, are you?

I'm Brigid Boszko and I'm here to look at a block of land – ten acres of well-earned escape that Rick and I are keen to find. I glance at the phone again: about half a k further along this track. We'll know what we're looking for when we see it – or I will. Rick is interminably tidying his desk in Sydney, before we can get out of there for good. Am I looking at our future now?

Guyong. Why do I think I recognise that name only now that I am sitting here stopped in the car on this track? I know Granddad grew up in the countryside somewhere past Bathurst – that'd be a hundred years ago, just about exactly – was it around here? Guyong. Yesterday, when I saw the property online, it seemed just another far-flung name that meant nothing to me, apart from the magic words of 'established trees', 'four bedrooms', 'two bathrooms' that came with it. Pretty pictures of a rambling old weatherboard homestead, not in need of renovations. Welcome to Wiradjuri Country, the sign back up on the highway told me. Hello? Something makes me want to know who and what lives here.

I pull the car over to the side of the road and get out. The sun is warm, the breeze is too, but my shiver deepens, plunging into the centre of me and swirling around. I'm excited, and I don't really know why.

It's probably just that we're so close now, to making this long string of wishes a reality. Finding our place, where I will write, and Rick will make his mad sculptures out of discarded engine parts, and we'll have a yard full of chickens and an orchard. And peace. The kids, Sam and Flynn, have grown and flown, and now it's our time to explore what we've always wanted to: each other, uninterrupted. Our friends think we've lost our minds. Shouldn't we be furiously working on our superannuation stockpile so that we can live out our days travelling the world? No.

We've done our travelling: separately and together. I've done the European tour three times – first, when I was twelve, that winter after Grandma died, that whole year I barely remember at all except as series of strange, dislocated postcards, then back again with Mum and Dad at seventeen, where I whinged the whole way through France and Italy, plagued by some mysterious adolescent malaise – both times missing out on getting to the promised lands of Poland and Ireland, because of a persistent Iron Curtain drawn down on one, and never-ending Troubles in the other. When Rick and I took the kids in 2007, Poland was too far out of our budget, too many miles away from London, where his cousins are, and Ireland was a melancholy detour from there. I dragged my little family to

Tralee, looking for the village Grandma was born in – Bally-something. I thought the name would come to me, once we were there, but it didn't. There are about fifty places starting with Bally in County Kerry and it could have been any one of them. In all the trivial and stupid things I've scribbled down throughout my life, I could have scribbled down that one important name, but I never did. And Mum wasn't here to ask, by that time.

Oh, Mum. I know she's really why I am standing here on the side of this dirt track, in this weird muddle of emotions. She died suddenly ten years ago, from an aggressive tumour in her stomach – cruel but quick. Terrifying. Dad couldn't cope: he died three years after her. He sat in front of the TV complaining about there being nothing on it: 'No stories, only blah blah blah, people yelling at you.' He sat there and stared at the yelling until he shrank into the lounge chair and faded away. They'd worked so hard all their lives, Mum and Dad – saving, saving, scrimping for their wonderful reward on retirement. They didn't get to enjoy it for more than six months.

It's not enjoyment I'm after, but work of a different kind. Work I've always wanted to do: to tell my own stories. These stories that whirl round my head, the rush of them getting wilder the older I get. I'm scribbling them down all the time, notes scrawled on post-its at the office, on the back of shopping dockets, tearing out pages from my kids' exercise books over the years. My laptop is stuffed with them: snippets, sketches, whole novels. I've even had a couple of them published here and there; one of them sold okay, too. But I want the time and the space now to let them come out as they will, not worked around other things, like drawing up contracts of sale on other people's properties, as I have done part-time and mindlessly for the past twenty-odd years to make a buck for our family business: Boszko and Braddon Conveyancing. That's not work: that's just marking off days. I have a lot to say before I die. I'm forty-seven: my life is at least half done, if I'm lucky. I need to make the last half count. I need this place – wherever you are.

Are you here?

'Bridge, you are nuts,' my brothers Shane and Tim say about our plans, but they've always said that about anything I do or am, haven't they. And they are tax accountants, both of them: they don't know life any other way. Money, money, money. When we were sorting out Mum and Dad's estate, they actually argued over the fair and proper distribution of the kitchen appliances. Seriously. 'But Bridge,' said Tim, 'if you retire early your kids will end up with nothing when you go.' They'll cope. Flynn is a lawyer, just like his pa, and Sam is just finishing up her degree in architectural design.

And I'm not retiring, thanks. Women don't retire: I see the old wax paper wrapper Grandma's circle bread used to come in, folded neatly by her kitchen sink, waiting to receive the day's garbage scraps, waiting there even on that day she died. Nothing wasted; not a moment, either, when it could and should be filled with love and care of some kind.

'You still doing your little writing thing?' an old girlfriend from those schooldays asked me a few weeks ago.

Yeah, my little writing thing. That, apart from my babies and my lover, means everything.

Everything.

Mum knew that. For all that we were never really mother-daughter close, not in that cheesy cheek-to-cheek way at least, she kept every scrap of every silly thing I wrote when I was a child: file after concertina file, the Z pockets at the back stuffed with doodles, odd little musings, on my revolting brothers, school, trains full of strangers, and Sharon who lived across the road, as well as a surprising number of grandly ambitious narratives mostly abandoned at around page three. My mother collected all of them, up until I turned twelve. Up until Grandma left us. I held my stories close after that. I don't think I wrote anything apart from a university essay then until I was about twenty-seven. Something in the bright-blue questions I found in my own children's eyes, something about their wonder at the world, started to bring my words back to me.

And now, just as I smile at the memory of my babies' always-asking eyes, something catches mine – a flash of blue in the tall grass ahead, over the other side of the track. It's a flower. I know as much about flowers as I do about farming – half a tick above nothing – but I know what this flower is. It's chicory.

Grandma. I know this is chicory because she told me. Because this is exactly what she described: a little piece of sky stuck high on a spindly stick of straw.

I start walking across the track and up towards this straw-stuck flower now. One of the cows at the fence lets out an almighty moo as I go, and I laugh as I look back over my shoulder at her big dark eyes following me. And when I look ahead again, beyond the rusting old hayshed, as the track bends and slopes gently away, I can suddenly see chicory everywhere. This lane is lined on both sides with sprinklings of sky.

All of my grandmother's stories tumble and spin through my heart at the sight. A tale of witches and fairies, foreigners and thieves; a distant crunch of wheels – going where? Her words flutter at the edges of my memory like butterfly wings, and I can't catch them.

But I will.

Here.

AUTHOR NOTE

Fact and fiction always play a merry game in my tales and *Wild Chicory* is no exception. I've thieved much of its truth and its heart from the lore of my Irish family – the Kellys and the O'Reillys – and I've pinched others from my husband, Dean's family, the Brownlees and the O'Brees, especially from Aunty Yvonne. The rest is blarney.

This is a story spun from my admiration for the economic refugees who have contributed to Australia from all over the world, all you brave wanderers, the ordinary hard-working dreamers who have made and continue to make our country what it is: a colourful patchwork of beauty and bigotry both, all sewn together with love. And no small part of its intricately crazed design is Irish. Indeed, Australia remains proportionately the most Irish country outside Ireland.

But most of all, *Wild Chicory* is the story of how

I came to be a writer myself, by the love of those who fed my soul their own stories when I was small, especially my grandmother, Lillian.

To those who have helped bring this story into the world, thankyou is never a large enough word. Lou Johnson, my original publisher, Alex Nahlous, my always excellent editor, my new Booktopia publishers, David Henley and Franscois McHardy, and my magical agent Selwa Anthony, this book wouldn't be here without you. And I wouldn't write any stories at all without my many comrades in words and my wonderful readers.

So, *slàinte*, friends – I hope you enjoyed the tale.

About the Author

Kim Kelly is the author of eleven novels, including the acclaimed *Wild Chicory* and bestselling *The Blue Mile*. With distinctive warmth and lyrical charm, her stories explore Australia, its history, politics and people. Her work has gained shortlistings in The Hope Prize and Australia's premier short novel award, Viva la Novella.

A long-time book editor and sometime reviewer, Kim is a dedicated narrative addict and lover of true love. In fact, she takes love so seriously she once donated a kidney to her husband to prove it, and also to save his life.

Originally from Sydney, today Kim lives in central New South Wales, on Wiradjuri country, with her muse de bloke, two cats and some chickens, and occasionally the kids when they come home to graze.